Jailed...

"There's a pay phone by the desk," he explained. "On our way out, you can call that pizza place out by where you're staying and order a large pepperoni pie."

The police technique must have worked. They'd driven her insane. She actually thought he'd said to order him a pizza.

"Come on, we'll pick it up on the way to your place."

"You're taking me home?" she asked.

"I didn't think you'd want to spend the night in a cell. So I've put you in my custody."

"*Your* custody? How can I be in anyone's custody? I haven't been arrested."

Creed nudged her forward again, his hand resuming its former place. "The only thing that stands between you and that little technicality—" he smiled, nodding acknowledgement to a passing officer "—is me."

Dear Reader,

Although our culture is always changing, the desire to love and be loved is a constant in every woman's heart. Silhouette Romances reflect that desire, sweeping you away with books that will make you laugh and cry, poignant stories that will move you time and time again.

This year we're featuring Romances with a playful twist. Remember those fun-loving heroines who always manage to get themselves into tricky predicaments? You'll enjoy reading about their escapades in Silhouette Romances by Brittany Young, Debbie Macomber, Annette Broadrick and Rita Rainville.

We're also publishing Romances by many of your all-time favorites such as Ginna Gray, Diana Palmer and Joan Hohl. Your overwhelming reaction to these authors has served as a touchstone for us, and we're pleased to bring you more books with Silhouette's distinctive medley of charm, wit and—above all—*romance*. I hope you enjoy this book, and the many stories to come.

Sincerely,

Rosalind Noonan
Senior Editor
SILHOUETTE BOOKS

CHRISTINE FLYNN
Stolen
Promise

Silhouette Romance

Published by Silhouette Books New York

America's Publisher of Contemporary Romance

To Roger with love.

SILHOUETTE BOOKS
300 East 42nd St., New York, N.Y.   10017

ISBN: 0-373-08435-8

First Silhouette Books printing May 1986

Books by Christine Flynn

Silhouette Special Edition
Remember the Dreams #254

Silhouette Desire
When Snow Meets Fire #254

Silhouette Romance
Stolen Promise #435

CHRISTINE FLYNN

admits to two obsessions: reading and writing, and three "serious" preoccupations: gourmet cooking, her family (she has a daughter and a husband she unabashedly describes as the sexiest best friend a girl could ever have) and travel. She tried everything from racing cars to modeling before settling into what she loves best—turning her daydreams into romance novels.

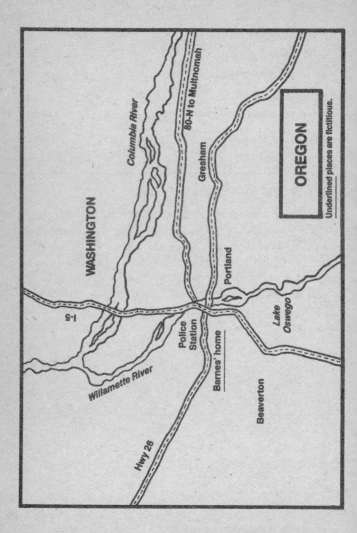

Chapter One

Britt raked her fingers through her long auburn curls—a gesture she had repeated often during the past three hours—and turned apprehensive brown eyes toward the uniformed officer perched on the edge of the table.

The officer's bland expression told her nothing.

If there was one thing she didn't like, it was not being in control of a situation. Lack of control frightened her. She was confused and, beneath her tenuous composure, she was also angry. Why wouldn't they believe her? She was innocent!

She, Brittany Elizabeth Chandler, a respectable art historian who in all of her twenty-five years had never had so much as a traffic ticket, was being held in an interrogation room at police headquarters—about to be charged with art theft.

"All right," the officer sighed, obviously growing as tired of the repetitive questions as she was. "Let's go through it one more time."

"Hold it, Johnson."

Britt glanced at the man leaning against the wall of the small, windowless room. One of the detectives who'd been in the room earlier had referred to the man simply as "Creed." Until now, the man called Creed had said nothing.

The detective had seemed surprised that Creed was still there, saying that he'd thought he'd left hours ago. Britt was convinced that the only reason he remained was to intimidate her. And he did. He would intimidate any woman and most men.

He was large. Not heavily muscled like the officer, but tall and powerfully lean. His curling black hair was as thick as the equally black mustache which all but obliterated a stern mouth. His nose was straight, though it looked as if it might once have been broken. But his most unnerving feature was the silver-blue eyes that never seemed to blink as he watched her from beneath a slash of ebony eyebrows. Even dressed in faded Levi's and the gray T-shirt molding the contours of his broad chest, he commanded more respect than the man in the uniform.

"Sir?" The officer swallowed, turning to the man who was apparently his superior.

Creed's eyes never left Britt's pale features. "Go see if the report's in on her yet."

His command met with immediate compliance.

As much as she'd wanted the questions to end, Britt would have preferred the officer's interrogation to being left alone with this man. He made her feel exposed and very vulnerable. She was used to the subtle, cultured masculinity of men whose interests lay in the arts and intellectual pursuit, not the raw, overpowering maleness that dominated Creed.

The first time she met Creed's eyes, she'd noticed an odd quickening in her stomach—that fluttery feeling becoming more pronounced when the light of a smile crept across his expression. His smile had vanished in the next instant, but the knot had remained.

There had been nothing overt about his silent assessment of her. But for the past hour, his gaze had seemed to linger on her mouth when she spoke, dropping every once in a while to the swell of her breasts beneath the black band of her white sundress. That look, though guarded with a mask of professional indifference, was pure male.

Unable to meet those penetrating blue eyes, she lowered her head to study the creases she'd pleated in her skirt.

"Just relax for a minute, Miss Chandler." Creed pushed himself away from the wall and lowered his formidable frame to the chair opposite where she sat at the table.

His words startled her, both by their quiet, soothing delivery and their ridiculousness. Relax? Impossible.

"Are they going to put me in jail?" The last word seemed to stick in her throat.

He said nothing for a moment as he studied her. Stress had removed the glow of her tan, turning her smooth skin ashen. And her dark brown eyes, their spark dulled by tension, appeared too large for the rest of her fragile features. She looked like an awed little waif hiding in a sophisticated shell.

Leaning forward, he reached for the pencil the officer had left on the table. "I want to see what the report says before I make that decision."

Britt tried to focus on what he'd just told her. *He* would make the decision. *He* was responsible for her fate.

But her attention was riveted to his hands. There was something vaguely sensual about the way his long fingers ran slowly up and down that pencil.

She forced her eyes to his face, attributing the tightness in her chest to nothing more than the strain she was under. "I've told you absolutely everything I know," she reiterated, refusing to allow her thin veneer of calm to crack. "I'm staying at the Barneses' home while they're in Europe on a buying trip. I had no idea the art they were sending back to the house was stolen. And I'm not guilty of anything."

"We hear that a lot around here."

"Well, in this case, it's true!"

A teasing light danced in his eyes. "We hear that a lot, too."

Sending him a glance of total exasperation, she leaned back in her chair. The smile that remained in his eyes was even more unnerving than the coolness. It made him seem more human and far too...attractive.

You're definitely losing it, she groaned to herself. They're about to lock you up for something you didn't do and you're sitting here thinking your potential jailer is attractive?

The door cracked open and a blue-sleeved arm motioned to Creed.

"I'll be right back." In one easy movement, he'd tossed the pencil aside and was on his feet. Quite unnecessarily, he added, "Stay here."

Where else could she go?

The minutes stretched into an hour. This must be part of their technique, she decided. Leave a person alone with their thoughts so they can go quietly insane. She must be halfway there already. Why else would she be wondering what Creed would look like without that mustache when she should be pounding on the door demanding to see a lawyer?

The door swung open and Creed's frame filled the narrow space. "Let's go."

Britt shrank back in her chair, unable to move. Was he going to book her now? Take her fingerprints and those awful mug shots that hung in every post office in the country? Oh, Lord! Her mother went to the post office by their summer home in Hyannis to pick up the mail. If she saw her only daughter's picture hanging in there, she'd have a stroke.

She saw Creed's chest expand with his heavy, indrawn breath and tried to disappear through the back of the chair when he moved toward her. He stood over her for a moment, indecision playing over his rugged features. Before Britt could even begin to hope that he might be releasing her, he reached down, cupped her elbows, and pulled her to her feet. "I said, let's go."

His hands felt hot against her skin and, as he lightened their pressure, his touch far too gentle. She decided it was only fear that made the knot in her stomach tighten. It couldn't possibly have anything to do with the fact that her fingers had just curled around his muscled biceps to keep from sinking through the floor.

"Are you trying to add assault to your charges?" With a quiet chuckle, he moved his thumb over the crease of her right elbow. "Your nails are punching holes in my arm."

Sucking in a quavery breath, she jerked her hands back. His grip fell away, which made her promptly drop back into the chair. She hadn't meant to sit down again, but her legs seemed to have lost a considerable amount of their stability. If he wanted to take her anywhere, he'd have to carry her.

The thought of his holding her, those strong arms pressing her against that rock-hard chest, only increased the arrhythmic pounding of her heart. "Don't I get a phone call or something?" she inquired with considerable aplomb. There was a lot to be said for remaining cool and calm in a crisis, even if she didn't feel anywhere near as calm as she sounded. Only years of rigid upbringing and her finely honed Boston reserve kept her from indulging in hysteria.

Her face was at eye level with his hips. Her throat went dry when she watched his hand disappear into the pocket of his jeans. The motion had pulled the already snug denim even tighter over the zipper.

"There's a pay phone by the front desk." He picked up her hand and folded a quarter into it. "You can call that pizza place on the highway out by where you're staying and order a large pepperoni."

Their technique must have worked. They'd driven her insane. She actually thought he'd said to order him a pizza.

"Come on." She was lifted from the chair again and guided through the door. "We'll pick it up on the way to your place."

"You're taking me home . . . to the Barneses'?"

"I didn't think you'd want to spend the night in a cell," he replied blandly, leading her down a labyrinth of brightly lit halls. "So I've put you in my custody." His hand slid to the small of her back, the warm sensation mingling with the jolt of his words.

"*Your* custody?" She stopped dead in her tracks. "How can I be in anyone's custody? I haven't been arrested!"

Creed nudged her forward again, his hand resuming its former place. "The only thing that stands between you and that little technicality—'' he smiled, nodding acknowledgment to a passing officer "—is me."

Where time had seemed to drag just a short while ago, things were now happening far too fast. They'd reached a large, open room filled with desks and a sea of blue uniforms. The room was dotted with an assortment of not-too-pleasant looking men and women whose occupations Britt didn't care to question. Creed was handed a brown leather garment bag by a grinning detective and seemed to be taking a lot of ribbing about something.

"It's no wonder they're promoting you," someone drawled from behind Creed. "I don't know of anyone else around here who'd spend his vacation trying to break a case."

"Open your eyes, man," came another voice. "This one appears to have some pretty compelling benefits."

The sting of heat rushed to her cheeks when the man's eyes wandered casually from the top of her head to her sandaled feet.

"Yeah, being single has its advantages. If he had a wife, he'd never get away with it." That came from behind an open newspaper.

"You be phoning in, Chief?"

"He won't be Chief until he gets back from vacation," someone drawled.

The way that last word was drawn out drew a hoot from somewhere in the back of the room.

Creed's voice sounded a little too low. "I told you where I'd be if you guys need something."

"Oh, right," the man who had asked the question replied. "Out at the Barneses' place."

Trying to move her between the desks, Creed received someone's good-natured punch in the arm with a grumbled, "Knock it off, Hollister," and, taking Britt by the hand, pulled her out into the night.

It was almost ten, and still warm outside. Only the breeze drifting across the Willamette River stirred the humid summer air engulfing the city of Portland. Britt was oblivious to the sticky heat. She didn't notice the lights of the bridge reflecting on the slowly moving river by the police station, or the tranquil rustle of leaves filtering through the distant sounds of the bridge traffic. She was conscious only of the man leading her down the long flight of steps and onto the sidewalk.

The thin fabric of her sundress tangled between her legs while she tried to keep up with his long strides. It wasn't that he was running. It was just that his legs were so long and, at five foot three, Britt's legs didn't cover quite the same amount of ground with each step. She wished he'd slow down. There were a few very specific questions she wanted to ask—starting with what that guy had meant when he'd said Creed was staying out at the Barneses'.

"Damn." Creed spun around so quickly that she collided with his shoulder. "Here." Steadying her before handing her a set of keys, he motioned toward the beige Seville parked at the curb. "Take this—" he handed her his garment bag "—and wait for me in the car. I was in such a hurry to get you out of there, I forgot about the pizza."

Before she could say a word, he turned and, taking the steps leading into the station two at a time, disappeared back through the glass doors.

"I don't believe this," she muttered, holding the bag against the car with her hip while she unlocked the door. The quarter she'd been clutching in her fist fell to the ground. Retrieving it, she pulled the door open, shoved his bag into the back seat, and tossed both the quarter and his keys onto the dashboard. "I really don't believe this," she repeated, and sank wearily into the passenger seat.

The rich scent of the leather interior mingled with a faintly spicy fragrance. His after-shave. She'd noticed it when he'd lifted her from the chair. Its spicy cleanness, heightened by the heat of his body, had been unsettling then and was even more so now. She couldn't explain why something so intangible should affect her at all.

It must be exhaustion, she told herself, casting a furtive glance back toward the station. Creed was coming down the steps. Seconds later, he'd opened the door and slid behind the wheel.

"Can I ask you what's going on?" She never had been one to sit and ponder when an answer was available.

Wryly eyeing the quarter on the dashboard, he picked up his keys and started the engine. "Sure."

"Well?"

"You asked if you could ask, and I said you could. Do you have another question?"

Patience, she admonished herself, glaring at him. She started to repeat what she'd just asked, then hesitated. She was almost afraid to voice the question uppermost in her mind, fearing that what she'd heard the man say about Creed staying with her might be confirmed. There was a more roundabout way of finding out what she wanted to know. "Did you reach Dr. Anderson and confirm what I told you?"

Lahrs Anderson was the distinguished head of the Masters' Program at the university Britt attended in Boston, and the person who had introduced her to John and Henrietta Barnes. The Barneses, apparently large contributors to the Alumni Fund, had needed someone

to house-sit while they were on their art-buying trip, and
Professor Anderson had thought it the perfect opportunity for Britt to complete her master's thesis.

"We reached him." Creed pulled the car out onto the
deserted street and headed for the freeway.

"And?" she prodded.

"It's part of the investigation." His oblique response
was evidently all the information she'd get on that subject. "What I want to know is whether or not you're
willing to cooperate."

"I already told you I don't want to have anything else
to do with this. All I want to do is go back to Boston and
forget I ever even met . . ."

"Look," he interrupted, glancing behind him to
change lanes. "You're not going anywhere. The position you're in, to put it mildly, is a little precarious.
You've received stolen goods *and* you've accepted payment for them. The way I see it, you can either cooperate as a private citizen and help me get evidence against
the Barneses or I can arrest you and you can help me as
part of a plea bargain."

Britt swallowed hard. "Didn't Professor Anderson . . . ?"

"Forget Anderson. Which way do you want it?"

What choice did she have? He obviously believed she
was guilty, and if helping him would get her out of this
mess . . . "I'll cooperate," she replied dully. "What do
you want me to do?"

She hadn't even noticed Creed's tension until she saw
his shoulders relax. Incredible as it seemed, she could
now almost hear a smile in his voice. "Nothing really.
Just do what you normally do. I'll stay with you and the
next time a delivery comes, you'll take care of it the way
Barnes has told you to."

"How long?"

"What?"

Watching the circles of light from the street lamps approach then disappear, she took a deep breath. "How long will you be staying?"

He didn't reply for a moment and Britt was acutely aware of his eyes on her. When he did speak, his deep voice was a little huskier, and quiet. "That all depends on you."

Something that felt like dread—or was it anticipation?—shuddered through her.

If only she'd been more like the rest of her family, she wouldn't be here now. She'd be either living in the gilded little world of garden parties and charity functions, like many of her married friends, or, like those who'd wanted a career and had joined the family business, be working for her father in his bank.

Britt, however, had always been a bit of a rebel. At least, she'd wanted to be. The staid and proper world of upper-crust Boston society held no enchantment for her independent spirit. Unfortunately, her inbred reserve didn't allow her to be completely unconventional. Art history could hardly be construed as a radical occupation, but it was something she'd chosen for herself, and not because it was expected of her.

A rebel. But a conservative one.

It was the rebel who now sat across from Creed in the large, modernized kitchen of the Barneses' palatial home, methodically picking the pepperoni from a slice of pizza she had no intention of eating. She was still upset, and very tired.

Creed didn't appear too interested in his dinner, either—though he'd insisted they eat before she showed him to the room he would stay in. Of the eight bedrooms in the house, Britt planned on putting him in the one farthest from hers.

Shoving her plate aside, she glanced at him. He was sitting with his arms folded across his chest, the bulge of his biceps straining against the constriction of his short sleeves. She knew he'd been watching her and his steady gaze had done nothing to improve her disposition. "Why won't you believe me?"

He held her challenging brown eyes evenly. "I haven't said I don't."

"Then you do?"

The little lines around those disturbing gray-blue eyes deepened with a barely suppressed smile. "I haven't said that, either."

Irritation flashed from between her thick lashes as she rose from the table. "Listen," she said, refusing to give in to her anger, which was no small feat considering her integrity was in question. "I'm not a criminal, nor am I a liar. If you knew me, you'd know I'm telling the truth and then none of this would be necessary." Her wadded up napkin was tossed on the table and she stood stiffly by the bay window. There was nothing to be seen in the night-blackened glass except her own agitated reflection—and Creed's quiet approach.

"That's exactly why I'm here." He stopped behind her. "It should be easy to get the evidence I need. Then, once I get to know you ..." The remainder of his words were expressed with a very unenlightening shrug.

Turning around, she tipped her head back to see his face. If she stared straight ahead, all she could see was his chest. "Then what?" she demanded.

"Then we'll just wait and see what happens."

Not once had he given her a straight answer, and something inside her snapped. "Are you going to tell me that for the next...for the next God-only-knows how long, you're going to be watching to see if I make any mistakes? Damn it!'' she seethed, not caring that her control had slipped. The strain of the past several hours had finally gotten to her. "I'm not some specimen you can put under a piece of glass. How can you expect me to act normally when I know you're watching every move I make? You already think I'm guilty and the only reason you're here is so you can prove it!"

"You said you'd cooperate."

His calm reminder, and the fact that he hadn't denied a thing she'd said, only increased her irritation. "If I don't?"

Immediately she regretted her challenge. It was obvious that she was verging on irrationality and she had to regain her composure before she wound up saying something really stupid.

Creed held her rebellious expression for several seconds before his softening gaze fell to her lips. "Then, we both might lose."

He might lose by not getting his evidence. She might lose by being arrested as an accomplice. Those were the logical conclusions to be drawn. But his eyes and the deep timbre of his voice told her he was talking about something else entirely.

She stood transfixed, her eyes locked on his, when he reached over and nudged an errant curl from where it had fallen against her cheek. Her eyes widened. She heard his quick intake of breath as his hand fell. She knew that the unexpected gesture had surprised him, too.

It was only by conscious effort that she kept her hand from covering the spot on her cheek where the warmth of his touch still lingered.

"You're tired," he observed quietly and shoved his hands deep in his pockets. "It's not going to do either of us any good to talk about anything tonight. I suggest you go to bed and, if you'll show me where you want me, I will, too."

She wanted him out in the garage. The Barneses had left her the keys to one of their cars, a little blue MG, but there was no way he could sleep in that. He might fit into the back seat of the Rolls-Royce parked in there though, if he could pick the lock.

Knowing he wouldn't appreciate her suggestion, she mumbled, "Come on," and turned off the lights to lead him past the dark rooms filled with antiques and imported rugs.

Creed shifted his garment bag higher on his shoulder when they reached the top of the ornately carved and curving staircase. "Where to?"

They were at the juncture of the east and west wings.

"You can have the last room on the right." She motioned to the east wing. "It's the one across from the master suite."

"Where's yours?"

"Down here." Expecting him to be going the other way, she headed down the west wing.

"I'll stay down here, too." He fell into step behind her. "Looks like there's plenty of rooms."

"I really think you'll be more comfortable..."

"...right here," he finished for her, opening the door across from hers. He flipped on the light and ducked his head inside. "This'll be fine."

Britt didn't trust herself to say a single word. Tossing him a mutinous glare, she turned on her heel and forced herself not to slam her door.

Never had she welcomed the sight of something so simple as a bedroom. Though the guest room with its gracious appointments lacked the familiar touches of her apartment back in Boston, it offered her the one thing she needed right now. Privacy.

Going through her usual routine of scrubbing off her makeup and applying the requisite strokes to her wildly curling hair—she'd tried everything to straighten it and finally resigned herself to being stuck with a mop of waving curls—she tried to sort through the confusion of the day's events. No amount of analysis could change the facts. She was suspected of a felony, and she had an honest-to-God cop living right here with her to prove it. The cop was the one thing she didn't want to think about.

The long navy blue nightgown she pulled over her head draped in a deep V over the points of her breasts and slid over the curve of her hips to the floor. Lifting a handful of the silky fabric, she crossed the blue and gray Aubusson rug to her bed, adamantly refusing to think about Creed.

Adamantly *trying* not to think about Creed, anyway. She couldn't help but wonder if that was his first name, or his last. She hadn't called him anything yet. "Creed." It had a good, solid ring. "Creed," she repeated, flipping back the satin bedspread.

"Britt? Are you decent?"

Her glance flew to the closed door, then down to her provocative nightgown. Grabbing the matching robe from the bed, she called, "Yes," and stuffed her arms into the flowing sleeves.

The door opened and he leaned against the frame. "There aren't any, uh . . ."

She'd just pulled the robe closed and her fingers were fumbling with the tie. His eyes darted from her flushed face to the skin exposed between her breasts. She'd forgotten that the cut of the robe matched that of the gown.

It took a visible amount of effort for him to look back up. "There aren't any sheets on the bed . . . and I need some soap."

She stifled the urge to say, "So?" and moved past him with as much dignity as she could muster. The appreciation in his eyes hadn't gone unnoticed and she wasn't about to stand around while he got an eyeful.

He was still in her doorway when she returned from the linen closet at the end of the hall. "Here," she said, handing him a set of sheets and a bar of soap.

He didn't move.

"Do you need something else?"

"Toothpaste. I was going to pick some up when I got to the hotel."

"The hotel?"

"I'm supposed to be on vacation."

She vaguely remembered having heard someone at the station mention that, but she didn't want to ask Creed about it. All she wanted was to escape back into her room. "I guess you'll have to use mine."

He shrugged. "What choice have I got?"

"That's the same question I've been asking myself," she mumbled, moving past him again and heading into her bathroom. Since all the bedrooms had adjoining baths, at least she didn't have to worry about sharing one with him.

His voice followed her. "What did you say?"

She could feel his eyes on her back. More specifically, on her bottom. "Nothing," she clipped, and returned seconds later to find him crossing her room.

He walked right past her and pushed the drapes back.

"It's two stories down," she advised him. "I'm not about to jump, if that's what you're thinking."

Ignoring her, he turned and then was on his knees beside her bed.

"What are you . . . ?"

Before the question was out, she had her answer. Winding up the cord of the phone on her nightstand, he disengaged the instrument and added it to his sheets and soap. Her teeth threatened to perforate her tongue when she handed him the crumpled tube she was holding.

He frowned down at the mangled toothpaste.

Britt frowned, too. "What's the matter?"

"You squeeze from the middle. You're supposed to squeeze it from the end."

She started to ask if that was a federal offense, but decided that under the circumstances, it wouldn't be wise. "I don't always do things the way I'm supposed to."

"I know," he said dryly, walking out before he could see how beautifully she handled that smug little crack.

Chapter Two

Britt usually awoke to the silence of the countrylike surroundings of the Barneses' stately home. Situated deep in the verdant Portland hills, its manicured lawns and formal gardens bordered by thick stands of oak and Douglas fir, none of the city sounds ever reached the idyllic setting. The intensity of that silence magnified the distinctive snap of the diving board at the pool behind the house.

It always took Britt forever to wake up. More often than not, she'd be halfway through her morning shower before the hazy fog would lift and her mind would begin to function. This morning, though, she was denied the luxury of not having to think.

Her first thought, unwanted as it was, was of Creed. Obviously he'd decided to go for a swim.

Sleep had taken the raw edge from her nerves. With the return of her composure had also come two resolutions. She would not lose her temper again—losing one's temper was certainly no way to prove one's innocence—and she would not let Creed's presence in this house disturb her.

The latter resolution lasted all of half an hour—from the time she made it while in the shower until she'd dressed and entered the kitchen. Both her resolve and the cup of tea she'd come for were forgotten with a slow blink of her lashes.

Creed was standing by one of the dark orange counters that formed a U around the stove in the center island. His back was to her and he wore nothing but a towel wrapped low on his hips. Beads of moisture clung to his broad shoulders and trickled down the indentation of his long back.

Her widening eyes followed the path of his spine to the tight outline of his lean buttocks. There was absolutely no indication that there was anything other than bare skin beneath that towel. Had he been swimming naked? She tried not to think about it while her eyes swept down to the dark hair curling against his muscular legs. His bare feet were leaving little puddles on the polished hardwood floor as he moved about the room, methodically going through every cabinet and drawer.

He turned to the cabinet over the built-in wine rack. Britt's gaze jerked up and glued to the perfectly formed pectoral muscles covered with a V of damp black hair that tapered down to meet the low-slung terry cloth.

Michaelangelo's *David*, she thought. Muscle and sinew sculpted to anatomical perfection. This man was not stone, though, he was flesh and blood and, unlike that master's perfect work of art, he was very real.

The room seemed to be getting rather warm.

You will not let his presence disturb you, she repeated to herself and moved to the counter dividing the breakfast nook from the spacious kitchen.

Her silent declaration was meaningless. His presence was extremely disturbing.

Irritated at having her resolve so quickly frustrated, she folded her arms over the yellow button-down blouse she'd tucked into her khaki skirt and fixed a quelling glare on the back of his head. "I thought you had to have a search warrant before you could start rummaging around." That was not the simple, civilized "good morning" she'd planned.

Creed didn't even look up before he bent to survey the contents of one of the lower cabinets. "I was wondering how long you'd stand there before you said something." The cabinet door banged shut. "All I'm looking for is coffee and scissors."

She didn't bother to question the strange combination, or to acknowledge any discomfort at having been caught gaping at him. Her preoccupation was with the towel that looked as if it had loosened a little when he straightened. "I don't have any," she returned, sharper than she'd intended.

Her legs felt shaky. Rather than trusting them to carry her any farther, she slid onto the nearest bar stool. It felt safer here. There was a whole counter separating them.

When he finally turned around, his eyes narrowed. "You don't have any scissors?"

Pulling out the drawer in front of her, she pushed a pair of scissors over the burnt-orange surface. "I mean I don't have any coffee. It has caffeine in it."

"I know." He raked his fingers through his still-damp hair, his expression one of decided indulgence. "That's why I want it."

"I've got some herbal teas." She really wished he'd do something about tightening that towel. "And there's fruit juice in the refrigerator."

With a resigned shrug, he padded through the puddles and took a bottle of orange juice from the fridge. Before closing the door he also extracted a carton of eggs and then stood scowling at the remaining contents. "Looks like you're out of bacon." He pulled out the two lower bins. "No sausage either?"

"I don't eat meat," she replied flatly, focusing on the row of copper canisters behind him. Looking at something inanimate seemed more prudent somehow—but not quite possible.

His eyes beseeched the ceiling. Britt thought she heard him mutter "Wonderful," while he opened the bread box.

"Whole wheat," he observed, setting the loaf next to the eggs. "I suppose you don't eat white bread?"

"Bleached flour doesn't have any bran in it." She stopped there, certain he wasn't interested in hearing about the rest of its deficiencies.

Leaning against the island, he crossed his arms over the breadth of his chest. Well-formed muscle glinted like hammered bronze as the shaft of light slanting through the window played over his shoulder. Though his mouth seemed set in annoyance, it was impossible to tell what expression really lurked beneath that mustache.

He probably has a weak upper lip, she thought absently.

"I suppose you don't use anything that comes prepackaged, either?" It was only the arching of his thick eyebrows that kept the question from sounding like a statement.

"Preservatives." She'd expected more questions this morning, but not about her eating habits.

"Do you subscribe to some abstract religion that prohibits normal things like steak or hamburgers, or do you just want to be different?"

He definitely had a way of shadowing his remarks. Somehow what he'd just asked didn't sound like an inquiry at all.

"I do it because I care about my health," she said with practiced calm. Treat arrogance with temerity and you always come out ahead. "Certainly you can understand that. After all—" a note of feigned sweetness entered her voice "—not everyone does laps at the crack of dawn."

"Eight o'clock is hardly the crack of dawn."

She met his eyes evenly, refusing to discuss something that was clearly a matter of opinion.

It wasn't annoyance she sensed in him now. Not with the way he was watching her. In his eyes was the unmistakable look of a man who clearly appreciated the attributes of the woman he was appraising. There was nothing veiled about the way his cool gaze moved from where she'd left the top three buttons of her blouse undone, and up to assess the generous curve of her mouth. His unnerving journey stopped briefly on the slight slant of her deep sable eyes—eyes that revealed a remarkable combination of poise and apprehension—then swept on to the shining mass of curls framing a face Britt knew was too thin to be called beautiful. She knew she was attractive, but she hardly thought of herself as someone who would cause men to drive into trees when they saw her walking down the street.

Creed's attention had returned to the provocative swell of her breasts. Apparently he didn't see any shortcomings.

He shoved himself away from the island, the lithe movement threatening to undo the towel completely when he moved toward her.

"Look," she began, rubbing her damp palms over her skirt and slipping from the stool to gain more distance. What was he going to do? "Why don't I fix you some breakfast while you go put some clothes on?"

That was not quite what she'd meant to say, but her thought had been verbalized before she could think of any other way to phrase it.

Creed must have found her reaction amusing. It appeared to take a lot of effort to hide the laughter curling the edges of his mustache. "Fine with me. Then, right after that—" he reached for the scissors he'd come for, the laughter glinting in his eyes when she took another backward step and bumped into the counter "—you and I are going to the store. You may be able to live on lettuce and carrots, but I can't."

Seconds later, she heard him bounding up the steps.

Britt didn't give any thought to what he was going to do with the scissors. She was too busy separating her relief from her irritation. Relief that he was finally out of sight, and irritation now directed at the water he'd tracked all over the floor. You'd think that a man who made such a big deal out of the proper way to squeeze a tube of toothpaste would be more careful about where he dripped.

Exactly fifteen minutes later, Creed's breakfast was ready. A fluffy omelet and a stack of wheat toast was waiting on the table in the bay-windowed breakfast nook. She started to fix herself a cup of tea.

One thing she was going to have to make clear was that this was a one time event. She wasn't going to cook and clean for him. She wasn't sure what the custodian-suspect relationship was supposed to be, but she wasn't going to wait on him hand and foot. That much she'd decided while on her knees mopping up the water he'd left on the floor.

"Smells good."

Her back was to him and she reached into the cabinet for a mug. "Do you want tea, or orange juice?" There was the tiniest bit of petulance in her tone. She didn't want it to be there, it just was.

"Orange juice," came his reply. A chair scraped against the floor and she knew he'd just sat down. "Where's yours?"

Closing the cupboard, she pushed a handful of hair behind her ear and turned around. "I don't usually eat break..." The other half of the word forgot to come out.

Over the counter separating them, she could see that he was dressed in a pale blue polo shirt. She could only assume it was tucked into something more substantial than the towel he'd been wearing.

But the mustache. It wasn't there anymore.

Deep, masculine creases were bracketing a firm mouth that was just beginning to show the first signs of a smile. His eyes, bright with taunting, lowered to his plate. "You say you don't usually eat breakfast?"

"Uh... no," she managed, returning her attention to the preparation of her tea.

She decided instantly that she preferred him with the mustache. Not because she'd found anything appealing about that untrimmed growth, but precisely because she hadn't liked it. Without even knowing why she felt the accusation necessary, she stated the obvious. "You shaved it off."

"You noticed," he returned blithely.

She couldn't help herself. She had to ask. "Why?"

"I didn't like it. The only reason I grew it in the first place was because I took a unit undercover on our last bust. Most of the guys grew full beards." With that semienlightening explanation, he shoved a forkful of omelet into his mouth. His brow immediately lowered. "Didn't you salt this?" Before she could answer, he held up his hand. "No. Don't tell me. You don't use salt, either. Right?"

A mischievous glimmer appeared in her eyes. "Wrong." Producing a box of salt, she sat it down in front of him. "I use it to kill slugs."

He never even blinked. "Guess I'll have to add homicide to your list of civil indiscretions." He added a sublethal dose of salt to his omelet. "Got any other skeletons buried in your closet?"

She met his teasing coolly. Giving her chin a defiant little tilt, she went back around the counter, reached for the skillet on the stove, and dropped it in the sink. Under no circumstances would she let him get to her. His presence was bad enough, but when he looked at her like that—like she amused him somehow—her control threatened to snap.

It was apparent enough that she wasn't going to answer and equally apparent that Creed wasn't going to accept silence. "Does this place come with a maid and butler?"

Briskly drying the copper skillet, she hung it on the circular rack above the center island. "A woman comes in to clean on Tuesdays, and the gardener shows up on weekends."

"You mean you have to do everything else yourself?"

"If by 'everything else' you mean my own cooking and laundry—" she stuffed the carton of eggs back into the refrigerator "—then, yes. Which," she added pointedly, "means you'll have to do the same." She held her breath, waiting to see what his reaction to that little proclamation would be.

"Won't bother me any. I clean up after myself all the time. Isn't it a little hard for you to get used to, though?"

She had to look at him, but his eyes were on the toast he held suspended between his fingers. "What's that supposed to mean?"

Crunching through the toast, he washed it down with a gulp of orange juice. "I just thought that having been raised as one of the idle rich, you might find it difficult...or maybe demeaning...to do such common things. You did give the officer your background yesterday. Remember?"

Oh, how well she remembered. She'd answered questions about everything from where she'd been born to how many times a day she left the house. About the only thing they hadn't asked was her blood type—and she wasn't so certain they hadn't found that out somehow.

"I told the officer I've been away from home since I went to college. And," she stressed, knowing he'd heard this all before because he'd been in the interrogation room most of the time, "that I've been supporting myself ever since. The money I'm living on now is what I earned before I quit the Smithsonian to go back to school. My savings are hardly enough to hire a maid."

"So you decided to supplement your income?"

His tone was deceptively bland, but Britt wasn't fooled for a minute. She knew exactly what he was alluding to.

Already on the defensive, she tried her best not to show it. "I'm staying here because I don't have to pay rent, and by subleasing my apartment I was able to save some money while I finished my thesis. That's the only way I'm 'supplementing' my income."

Presenting her back to him, she turned to the sink.

"What made you decide to go back to school?"

"I want to teach." Turning on the faucet, she glanced over her shoulder and turned it off again. "Teaching children about their heritage isn't illegal, is it?"

Creed ignored the question. "I thought art history was your major."

"It is. But one way of learning to appreciate history of any kind is through art." Not wanting to get on her soapbox, she told herself he'd get one more observation then she'd drop the subject. It would probably bore him to death anyway. "Children respond to pictures and things they can touch and feel in a way they can't to something they read in a book."

A thoughtful frown touched his forehead. "How do you know that?"

"I saw it when I worked with the school kids who toured the Smithsonian," she explained, putting the bread away.

"You like kids?"

Not trusting the reason for his question, though it was probably asked just for the sake of conversation, she turned the water on again. "They're all right," she said, unable to keep the wistful note from her otherwise terse response. She adored children and despite the way society frowned on large families, that was exactly what she wanted someday. Of course, there was first the matter of finding a man she could love for the rest of her life—not that she was looking at the moment. Then, there was this new turn of events to consider. Both her career and her future family could remain nothing but dreams if she wound up in jail.

Creed was smiling at her understatement. "Are you always in such a pleasant mood in the morning?"

"There's nothing wrong with my mood." Nothing that the absence of you and this whole ludicrous situation wouldn't cure, she added silently. She should have him clean this mess up. After all, it was his breakfast.

"I take it you didn't sleep very well last night."

He was smiling. She could hear it in his voice. The last thing she was going to do was confirm it by looking at him, though. Every time her eyes met his, all she could see was the terribly attractive man whose simplest gesture seemed to play utter havoc with her sensibilities. There was no doubt in her mind how the men who'd come up against Mata Hari must have felt.

A glass slid through her soapy hands and bounced against the rack in the dishwasher. It didn't break, and she wedged it in place more carefully. If he'd just stop watching her, she wouldn't have so much trouble functioning. "Is that an official question?"

"So," he drawled, picking up his plate to carry it to the sink. "That's what's bothering you."

The second he stopped beside her, she grabbed the sponge and moved to the stove to clean it. That tactical maneuver didn't do a bit of good. About three seconds later he was standing next to her, and she forgot to watch what she was doing. The sponge slid from her fingers and as she tried to grab it; the side of her hand hit the burner. She'd been so preoccupied before that she'd forgotten to turn it off.

Inhaling a sharp gasp as her hand jerked back, she stared down at the reddening flesh. "Now look what you made me do!"

Not dignifying her blurted words with a response, Creed grabbed her wrist and hauled her to the sink. "Hold still!"

"It hurts!"

"Of course it does, and it'll hurt a lot more if you don't get the heat out of it. Stop pulling away like that."

Britt didn't doubt for a second that he was accustomed to having his commands obeyed. But to reinforce his order and keep her from moving, he pressed himself against her back, still holding her hand under the water.

The burning in her hand was forgotten. The heat of his body was definitely more disturbing.

"Now, what did you mean by saying I made you do this?"

She could hardly tell him that every time he got within six feet of her she lost all ability to function, so she just muttered, "Nothing."

An unintelligible oath was mumbled over the top of her head. She didn't ask him to repeat it.

"It's better now." She hoped the tremors chasing each other from her neck to her toes weren't evident in her voice.

"Give it another minute."

Another minute? Another sixty seconds of having to feel his chest pressing to her back, the hard flatness of his stomach molding to her hips? Her heart wouldn't hold out that long! "Really," she breathed. "It doesn't hurt any more."

"Are you sure?"

"Very."

Reaching over her shoulder to turn off the faucet, he picked up the towel from the counter and turned her around. She couldn't have pulled away now if she'd tried. Her legs felt as if they'd just taken root in the floor. Fascinated with his gentleness, the way he cradled her hand in his large palm and almost delicately dabbed away the last drops of moisture, she tipped her head back to look at him.

Concern was etched deeply in his face. His mouth, a very sensual mouth she decided, was held in a tight line as he continued his ministrations. Who would ever have thought that someone this overwhelmingly male could be so tender?

A twinge of remorse vied with other less definable feelings. It hadn't been his fault she'd been so inept. He didn't know how he affected her—nor would he if she had anything to say about it—so how could she blame him? She hadn't even realized how tense she'd become until her groundless accusation had slipped out. It wasn't *his* fault he had to be here. "Thank you," she offered quietly.

The towel was back on the counter and her hand was dry, but he wasn't letting go. Warily, she glanced back up. There was nothing to be read in his expression now. No concern. No teasing. No coolness. Whatever was there was shuttered from her.

The spiky fringe of his dark lashes narrowed. The way he considered her seemed remote, yet oddly intimate. His gaze drifted to her mouth.

She knew she should say something, do something. It was not only dangerous, it was downright stupid to be standing here wondering what his lips would feel like against hers. It was obvious enough that that same thought was going on in his mind.

Britt started to speak, but nothing came out.

Creed's glance lowered and he ran his finger lightly around the pinkish burn. "I'm sorry about your hand." Her skin tingled where he touched it. Her skin tingled in places he hadn't touched. "Does it feel better?"

Still she couldn't speak. She just nodded, the motion brushing the cascade of auburn curls over her shoulders. Why did it seem so hard to breathe?

"You'll have to be more careful," he advised quietly.

Fear. That's what had just made her stomach ball up in a neat little knot. The kind of fear that comes with the beginnings of an attraction that has to be avoided—and the awful feeling you might not be able to avoid it.

Yes. She'd definitely have to be careful.

She slowly withdrew her hand, her head lowering to follow its descent. "If you don't need me to answer any questions right now, I think I'll go work in the study." She'd found her voice, but it sounded weak to her ears.

"Look at me, Britt."

Reluctantly, she did—and immediately wished she hadn't. His easy smile was totally disarming.

"I want you to promise me something."

Her brow furrowed. "Promise you what?"

"Oh, don't look so suspicious," he chuckled, crossing his arms. "I just want you to promise me you'll forget why I'm here."

He had to be crazy—or terribly devious. "I'm afraid that's not possible." Or, she added to herself, advisable.

"Okay," he conceded. "Then just promise me you'll try."

"Why?"

"Because I think it'll make things easier for both of us."

"How?"

His features relaxed in indulgence. "Because then you won't be so nervous, or so suspicious of anything I ask . . . and I won't have to worry about getting guarded responses from you."

"All the easier to trap me?"

Indulgence was being forced out by exasperation. "*That* is exactly what I'm talking about. I don't want you trying to find ulterior motives behind my every question. Or action," he added, a little quieter. "I want you to forget why I'm here and just be yourself."

She hadn't been herself since she'd opened the door on the two policemen who'd come for her yesterday.

Of all the things he'd just said, the word he'd spoken so quietly was the one she suspected most. "What do you mean by not wanting me to find any ulterior motives behind your actions?" Was he going to have the place bugged or something? "What are you going to do?"

Pure devilry lit his eyes as he crossed the little bit of distance she'd managed to put between them. Ever since she'd regained possession of her hand, she'd been edging backward. "I hadn't planned on doing anything, just yet. But since you obviously don't like being left in the dark," he continued, trapping her between him and the counter, "I'd be more than willing to tell you what I'd planned on doing later. Or would you prefer I just show you?"

There was no mistaking his intent. Britt pressed herself flatter against the surface behind her and silently damned herself for being so blasted inquisitive. "I think I'd prefer that you just tell me."

"You sure?" With one finger he tilted her chin up, his thumb moving over the fullness of her bottom lip. "They say that actions speak louder than words, you know."

I know! I know! her mind shouted. He was going to do exactly what she'd been thinking about just a minute ago. "I think I'd really rather . . ."

The pressure of his thumb against her lips silenced her.

The knot in her stomach must have spawned a clone. There was another one in her throat and the lump grew larger when she saw his dark head descending.

His mouth hovered inches above hers, his warm breath teasing her cheek. "You're not afraid of me, are you?"

Yes! something in her heart screamed. "No," she breathed.

"I don't want you to be afraid." His words were nothing more than a whisper. "Are you sure you just want me to tell you?"

Defiance was about the last thing she could manage with any conviction right now, but it was certainly worth a try. She practically swallowed a tight little "Yes."

A soft smile crept into his eyes. "Have you always been this stubborn?"

Lost in the depths of his gentle gaze, she didn't even realize she'd nodded.

His smile deepened and his head inched lower. "I can be very stubborn, too."

And determined, she thought.

The cool firmness of his mouth barely touched hers, the sensation no more than the tiniest brush of a feather. He pulled back just far enough to whisper, "Kiss me, Britt."

She couldn't help herself. Like the moon pulling the tide with its invisible force, something was drawing her toward him. So strong was the subtle power he was exerting over her that she couldn't even question what she was doing. Her lips, softly parted, met his.

There was no urgency. Creed's mouth moved slowly against hers, savoring the feel of her own lips. Then, more surely, he coaxed her lower lip with the tip of his tongue, gliding behind the warm inner membrane and tracing the same slow path along the top.

Only his hand, cupping her face, and his lips, touched her. Instinct made her want to move closer, to have the contact he was deliberately denying. Britt's fingers curled at her sides to keep from reaching up and winding around his neck. He tasted hot and sweet, and something hot was forming inside her.

His hand slipped to her throat when he raised his head. The lazy smile curving his mouth did nothing to hide the desire in his eyes. "Would you like me to explain further?"

The husky question was barely audible. Britt didn't know if it was because he was whispering, or because the pounding in her ears was making it so difficult to hear. She tried to lower her head. His thumb under her chin prevented it. "I don't think it's necessary."

"You said you weren't afraid of me," he reminded gently.

She wished she wasn't so short. Or maybe she wished he wasn't so tall. Whichever it was, she wished she could meet him at eye level so she wouldn't feel at such a disadvantage. "I'm not," she lied, averting her eyes from his.

There were a few strands of silver nestled in his sideburns. Funny, she hadn't noticed them before. Odd that she should notice them now.

The slight pressure of his thumb drew her glance back to him. "Will you give me that promise?"

Promise? she echoed silently. Her mind didn't seem to want to function. Nothing seemed to be working properly. Least of all her legs, which should be carrying her somewhere—anywhere—else.

Then she remembered. He wanted her to promise that she'd forget why he was here. For the last few irrational seconds, she actually had.

Then she remembered something else. He'd worked it so she was the one to kiss him. He already thought she was a liar and a thief. Hard telling what he thought of her now. "No," she returned flatly. "I think we'd both better remember exactly why you're here." Didn't she have a big enough problem as it was, without letting things get more complicated? What was the matter with her anyway?

Maddeningly enough, he didn't seem at all displeased with her pronouncement. "I have no intention of forgetting why I'm here," he said smoothly, running his thumb over her jaw. The sensation was far more pleasant than Britt was willing to admit. "Like I said before, I can be very stubborn, too."

Dropping his hand just as she twisted her head away, he moved toward the sliding glass doors leading to the pool. "Let me know when you're ready to go to the store. Just make it sometime before lunch, okay?"

"I don't want to go to the store."

He stopped in midstride and turned around. His hands were planted on his hips and with the morning sun pouring through the tall glass doors, he appeared as a formidable shadow against the brightness. "I didn't ask if you wanted to go," he clarified mildly. "I'm not going to leave you here alone and if I say you're coming with me, you will. Understand?"

She had no choice, and the total lack of control she now had over her life finally hit her. They may not have put her behind bars, but she was just as surely a prisoner. And the man whose touch had unlocked a Pandora's box of emotions—the man who was here to prove her involvement in the Barneses' illegal transactions—was just as surely her warden.

Rebellion etched firmly in her dark and fiery eyes. He'd made his intentions clear enough and there was no way she was going to provide him with a little diversion while he tried to prove her guilt.

She was about to tell him that when the shrill ring of the telephone cut her off. Putting all the indignation she was feeling into her action, she grabbed for the wall phone hanging beneath the cabinet. Creed's hand landed on top of hers a split second later.

How could a man move so fast?

Giving the receiver a jerk, a little surprised that she'd managed to get it away from him, she put it to her ear. "Barneses' residence," she answered, glaring at him.

The terse male voice on the other end of the line asked to speak to Captain McAllister. She started to say there was no one there by that name when it hit her. He wanted to talk to Creed.

So that was his name. Creed McAllister.

The pinched line of her mouth grew tighter. Acting as if this was the only way she could avoid her growing panic. "It's for you, *Captain*."

Chapter Three

"Are you really working in here . . . or just hiding?"

Creed leaned negligently against the door of the study, his cryptic expression falling on Britt, who sat behind the heavy antique desk pretending concentration.

Hiding, she admitted to herself. "Working," she told him, not taking her eyes from the page she'd been staring at for the better part of the morning.

For the past two days she'd spent all but a few of her waking hours hibernating in this rather ostentatious room. The floor-to-ceiling bookcases were filled with priceless rare works, many of those volumes divulging precious bits of information that she was incorporating into her thesis. Or trying to, anyway. Too many other thoughts were slowing down her progress, such as those centered around the owners of this house. She knew only what Professor Anderson had told her about them, which had seemed enough at the time. "Fine, upstanding members of the community," he'd said, "who need someone they can trust to take care of their home while they're away and to handle the art they'll purchase and ship back. Can't go carting priceless paintings all over Europe, you know.'' That had made sense to Britt, and the Barneses had seemed awfully nice when she'd shown up on their doorstep after the Professor had made the arrangements.

Though she'd been a bit overwhelmed at Henrietta's size—the woman had to be close to six feet tall and the tight bun of her mousy brown hair did little to soften her rather harsh appearance—Britt had thought her manner quite pleasant. No particular impression of John Barnes had really ever formed. The gray-haired gentleman, whose head almost reached his wife's shoulder, had said little while Henrietta gave Britt a quick tour of the house, opening his mouth only to mutter something about being late.

They certainly hadn't seemed like thieves. But, then, she really didn't know what a thief was supposed to be like. She had about as much experience with that particular element of society as she did with the police, and Creed didn't quite fit into his category, either. Even while castigating herself for not getting more information before coming here, she noticed that thoughts of his puzzling behavior since that first morning kept intruding.

He'd made no attempt to question her about her involvement with the Barneses. And, as grateful as she tried to convince herself that she was, she was surprised that he hadn't made a single attempt to touch her. If it hadn't been for the fact that she could hear him pick up one of the extensions every time the phone rang, she might not have known he was there at all.

He may have been staying out of her way, but she hadn't forgotten for an instant that he was there, and why. Apparently he was just waiting—waiting for the call Mr. Barnes would make to tell Britt another package was being shipped to the house. That certainly explained why he listened to her phone conversations. Not that there'd been anything incriminating about the call she'd received from the cleaning lady who was down with the flu, or the library telling her that they'd been unable to locate the book she'd requested.

Creed moved noiselessly across the rich reds and blues of the Sarouk rug. "Don't you think we need a break?"

Shoving back a handful of hair, the slats of light filtering through the walnut shutters touching points of fire to its silken curls, she met his enigmatic eyes. "I'm not sure what you need a break from," she returned, ignoring the flutter of pulse that came with predictable regularity every time she saw him. Did he know she watched him through the slit of her curtains when he did his laps in the morning? She didn't think so. He would have commented on it by now. He seemed unnervingly aware of her every move. "Unless," she continued blandly, "you consider lying by the pool while you read the paper or being on the phone hard work."

He shrugged. "I'm on vacation," he said, and lowered himself into one of the oxblood leather chairs in front of the desk. Stretching his denim-covered legs out in front of him, he crossed his arms over his light brown tank top.

He either works out at home or at some club, she thought, wishing at the same time that he'd just go away. Or maybe the police station had a weight room. A man simply was not born with shoulders, biceps and a chest like that, and a man his age—she'd finally decided he must be in his late thirties—had to do something to maintain such a physique.

Realizing that she was staring at the ebony hair swirling above the edge of his shirt, and refusing to be embarrassed by her open appraisal—art in all its forms was to be appreciated, wasn't it?—she met his eyes with deceptive coolness. "I thought you were supposed to be conducting an investigation."

"I am."

"By the pool?"

"On the phone. You could join me, you know."

"On the phone?" she returned dryly.

His expression was lenient. "By the pool."

"I don't think so."

"Why not?"

"Because I don't want to."

"Don't want to?" His penetrating eyes pinned her with their all-too-knowing gaze. "Or are afraid to?"

His powers of perception were maddeningly keen.

She would have loved to spend her afternoons lying by the pool. Being cooped up in the house all day was beginning to make her feel like a mole, and the tan she'd acquired in the month she'd been here was already starting to fade.

Sacrificing a tan was preferable to enduring the subtle, indefinable tension that crackled between them whenever they occupied the same space, though. The very air she breathed seemed to change consistency whenever he was around. "That's ridiculous. I've just got other things to do, that's all."

"Like gazing at the same piece of paper you were staring at when I came in here yesterday morning?"

The man was far too observant. A result of his occupation, no doubt. The sheet lying on the desk in front of her *was* the same one she'd been holding when he'd walked in yesterday, placed a tall glass of iced herbal tea beside her, said, "I thought you might want this," and left.

The gesture had puzzled her. As had his actions last night when she'd fallen asleep on the tufted leather sofa behind the desk. She'd awakened to find the wedding ring quilt she'd been piecing together folded up on the end table and a blanket carefully placed over her. She could find no motivation for his thoughtfulness.

She didn't want him to be thoughtful. She wanted him to be nasty and crude and condescending and all those other abhorrent things the super-macho cops she'd seen on television seemed to be. It would also help matters considerably if he wouldn't look at her like this. He appeared quite preoccupied with the golden expanse of her shoulders, bared except for the two tiny straps holding up the bodice of her powder-blue sundress. His eyes slid lower and the gauzy fabric suddenly felt too thin. She put her hand to her throat, her attempt to block his view anything but subtle.

"While you're trying to think of all those 'other things' you have to do," he mocked softly, "we'll go for a ride." Reaching across the desk, he pushed the page to the center of the blotter. "It'll be right here waiting for you when we get back."

"I don't want . . ."

"You don't need to tell me you don't want to go." His interruption was as smooth as the movements bringing him to stand next to her. "I'm going for a ride, and you're coming with me. Now, are you going to get up by yourself, or do I have to help you?"

Remembering the last time he'd pulled her from a chair—the feel of those strong arms lifting her so effortlessly—she rolled the chair back and stood up. She wasn't going to give in quite yet, though. "Aren't you afraid of missing Mr. Barnes's call?"

Britt was just as anxious for that call to come as she thought Creed was. Listening to that conversation should prove to him that she had nothing to do with the Barneses' scheme. Mr. Barnes would just tell her how much she was to collect for the painting or sculpture he was shipping, when the buyer would drop by to pick it up—the gallery he owned was closed while he and his wife were in Europe and he'd told Britt that these were his "special" customers—and then he'd ask if everything was all right with the house. If she was a co-conspirator, the conversation wouldn't be so straightforward and there would undoubtedly be some discussion of the illegal activity. She'd said as much to Creed on their way back from the store—one of the few things she had said to him the remainder of that first day—but he hadn't commented on her logic. All he said was that she was to keep Barnes on the phone as long as possible. When she'd then asked if it was possible to trace transatlantic calls, assuming that's what he wanted to do, he'd just given her a strange little smile and changed the subject.

To Britt, everything hinged on that call.

Creed edged forward. "If he doesn't reach you, I'm sure he'll try again later."

The back of her knees hit the chair when she moved an equal distance away. "Don't you think it would be better if we waited?"

"It's not something we're going to discuss. We're leaving in five minutes."

His hand lifted as she started to step in front of him and her heart jumped to her throat. He wasn't reaching for her though. The instant his hand curled over the telephone, she scooted to the door. "Close it behind you," he clipped, not bothering to look up before he began punching out numbers.

His conversations always took place behind closed doors. That was one of the only two rules he'd laid down to her. The other was that she was to tell no one who he was or why he was there. The cleaning lady and gardener could be dealt with easily enough and, since Britt didn't know anyone else in Portland, there was no one to tell. Even if there had been, it wouldn't exactly be to her benefit to broadcast the fact that she was suspected of a felony.

Though she was undeniably curious about his phone calls, it never occurred to her to try to listen in on them. Her innate respect for privacy prevented it. She would obey his rules.

Without asking herself why she was bothering, she ran her brush through the layered curls of her hair and checked the makeup which, for some unknown reason, she'd spent an inordinate amount of time applying this morning. There was no time to change and she wasn't about to risk aggravating Creed. She'd save any show of defiance for when it might really count.

Stubbornness didn't always have to be a liability. Her determination was being used now to check any action that might make her appear uncooperative—or betray the intensity of the attraction she was busily trying to deny. If he wanted to go for a drive, then they'd go for a drive. And she'd be ready in the ridiculously short time he'd alloted her. Just like a good little prisoner.

Complacence never did sit well with Britt.

The frown creasing her forehead deepened when she reached the stairs and started down. Creed was pacing over the marble floor of the entry, alternately glancing at his watch and then back at the stairs. He stopped when he saw her, impatience stamped on his dark and brooding features. He seemed awfully annoyed and in a very big hurry.

"Come on." Jerking the front door open, he motioned her toward it. "Let's go."

Puzzled rather than irritated by his imperious demand—and maybe a little intimidated by the sudden change in his manner—she ventured hesitantly, "I have to lock up first. If you'll give me a minute, I'll..."

"I've already done it." He took her by the arm and propelled her out the door, not releasing his impersonal grip until she was seated in his car.

Britt looked up, warily regarding the rigid set of his jaw. "Is something...?" The door was closed before she could finish her question. She decided not to repeat it when he got in, slammed his door, and pulled the car out of the circular drive. It was a dumb question anyway. Of course something was wrong. But what?

Whatever it was apparently had something to do with that last phone call. Unable to imagine what could possibly have put him in such a black mood, she arbitrarily decided he must have been talking to a girlfriend. After all, he had to have at least one somewhere. It was absurd to think a man like him would live the life of a monk.

The funny ache in her stomach must be indigestion, she thought. It couldn't possibly be jealousy.

They were ten minutes away from the house before Creed broke his preoccupied silence. "Have you ever seen Multnomah Falls?"

A chameleon couldn't change colors as quickly as Creed had. Moments ago, he'd been so absorbed in whatever it was he'd been thinking about. Now every trace of his preoccupation was gone.

She shook her head in response to his question, indicating that she hadn't.

"Then prepare yourself to see some of the most fantastic scenery in the world . . . other than that occupying the seat beside me, I mean."

A playful smile lit his eyes and she looked away. If he was trying to keep her off balance, he was definitely succeeding. Deciding to ignore the blatant compliment, she kept her tone guarded. "The world's an awfully big place for you to make a statement like that."

"I've seen enough of it to know fantastic when I see it."

Was he talking about scenery, or her? She didn't ask. Instead, she opted to satisfy her curiosity about him. "Just how much of it have you seen?" She had no idea how much a police captain—soon to be Chief, if she'd understood that officer's remark at the station correctly—received for a salary, but she didn't think the amount would allow for trips to many exotic places. On the other hand, he could obviously afford this new Seville. Perversely, she wondered if he accepted bribes.

Intuition told her he was too honest for that.

Creed laid his arm over the seat back, the relaxed curve of his fingers inches from her neck. "Just Europe and South America." Seeing her blank look of incomprehension, he added, "My father's with the Foreign Service. He's an ambassador."

His abstract tone indicated that he wasn't at all impressed with his background. Britt, though, was quietly amazed at his revelation.

"What's your mother?" She told herself not to be surprised if he said she was the former Queen of Siam.

"An ambassador's wife," came his bland reply.

That was more of what she might expect from him. A little old-fashioned chauvinism. Somehow it made him fit the mold of hard-bitten cop a little better. "I see," she pronounced flatly.

"No, I don't think you do." He chuckled and wound a soft curl of her hair around his finger. "Mom is quite content raising dad. She says it's the only occupation she'll ever find where she can really use her degree in psychology."

An unwilling smile tugged at her mouth. She didn't know why, but she felt a certain sympathy for Creed's mother—especially if father was anything like son.

Creed was still toying with the shiny curl at the back of her head. The motion was so absent that Britt wasn't sure he was even aware of what he was doing. Not wanting to break his mood, fearing he might revert to his former stony silence, she tried to ignore the harmless, yet oddly intimate gesture. "Where are your parents?"

"In Zurich. That's where I'm supposed to be now."

His eyes were on the road, his finger winding and unwinding the auburn tendril. Nothing in his too-perfect profile—even the slight irregularity of his nose couldn't mar the chiseled symmetry—indicated displeasure over the fact that his vacation had been forfeit to his desire to break a case.

Though he seemed quite at ease, Britt wasn't. "Have you always been so dedicated?"

The edge in her voice drew his eyes to her, but she kept her gaze straight ahead. "What do you mean?"

"Obviously proving my guilt is more important to you than seeing your family. I was just wondering if you've always been so devoted to your job."

The hand that had been getting awfully close to her cheek joined the other on the steering wheel. Despite the

way the muscle in his jaw jerked, his voice was even.
"I'm not going to comment on your first observation.
And, yes, my job is important to me. It's been important enough that I've put off doing a lot of things I've
wanted to do... like settling down to have a family until
I knew my work wouldn't interfere with my personal life.
But what's more important is that I always get what I'm
after." IIis hands eased their stranglehold on the wheel,
and Britt could feel his eyes on her. "I'd just appreciate
it if you'd make it a little easier."

There was no doubt in her mind that he always got
what he was after. He seemed every bit as stubborn and
determined as she'd ever thought of being. But he'd have
a battle on his hands this time. Why should she help him
prove her guilt? She was trying to prove her innocence!

Remembering that, and the promise she'd made to
herself that she would not lose her composure again, she
tilted her head toward him.

He was smiling! Did the man think this was all some
big joke?

"I'm doing all I can to cooperate with you, Captain."
Her tone was admirably quiet. She would not lose control! "And when you find out how wrong you are, I hope
you choke."

At her rather elegant delivery of her wish, Creed's
smile widened to a full-blown grin. He started to laugh.
A deep rich laugh that filled the interior of the car with
its beautiful sound.

"What's so funny?" she demanded, indignant.

"You are, honey," he said, his eyes dancing over her
frustrated features. He lifted her hand and pressed a kiss
into her palm. "You are," he repeated, placing her hand
back in her lap.

Britt was rarely at such a loss for words.

Curling her fingers over her palm, the skin there feeling warm where he'd kissed it, she fixed a determined stare out the window. His actions and his words had completely disarmed her, and she needed to regroup. If it hadn't been for the bizarre set of circumstances surrounding them, she knew she could find herself caring very much for this man. Maybe she already did. A little.

Not wanting to dwell on that quagmire of ambivalent emotion, she forced herself to concentrate on the view unfolding around them. If he wanted her to see scenery, then she'd see scenery.

The intention was there, even if the fact was not. Just as they had for the past two days, unwanted thoughts of Creed kept intruding on her concentration. She wasn't really seeing the verdant hills rolling along the banks of the Columbia River. She barely noticed the cool blues and greens of the water melding with the deeper loden and emerald of land to meet a sky so clear its color rivaled anything on an artist's palette. Even Renoir couldn't have captured the elusive play of the sun on the sometimes turbulent, sometimes placid river. Normally, she would have found the quiet beauty of the Columbia Gorge awesome and peaceful, but peace was one feeling she couldn't fathom at the moment. Not with Creed sitting beside her.

"It's really something, isn't it?"

His voice drew her from her troubled thoughts, the motion of his hand adding to the distraction. For a moment she thought he was reaching toward her, but he only withdrew a cassette from the glove compartment and slipped it into the tape deck.

He must have meant his question only as an observation not requiring a response. Seconds later the familiar strains of a Strauss waltz filled the car, the clear melody a perfect counterpoint to the lush beauty surrounding them.

The slight lift of an eyebrow was the only indication of approval Britt allowed herself. His taste in music also surprised her. She found herself wondering if, as a young boy who'd been raised in diplomatic circles, he'd been weaned on the classics as she had. But she didn't ask. The less she knew about him, the less she'd have to forget. After all of this was over—providing she didn't spend the next ten years in Leavenworth—she'd go back to Boston and hope no one at any of the elementary schools she'd applied to had any gossipy relatives working for the Portland police. Creed would probably forget she'd ever even existed. She'd have just been another suspect in a long list of cases.

An aching little void encroached upon that thought.

Multnomah Falls was, indeed, spectacular. Standing on the bridge spanning the tree-enshrouded pool below, watching yet another fall of rushing water rumbling from that pool to another beyond, Britt leaned against the gray concrete rail. "It is fantastic," she sighed. Her gaze had been drawn to the top of the falls some six hundred feet above.

Expecting Creed to deliver a well-earned "I told you so," she turned to receive it. She'd felt him watching her, but until now she hadn't realized how intent his scrutiny had been.

"I agree," he returned, touching one of her mist-spangled curls. His features drew together in thoughtful contemplation. "Did you know that when the sun hits your hair like this, it looks like there's a thousand little jewels in it? Almost like blood rubies and topaz?" His blue eyes, dark now like the water at the edges of the pool, were on the curl he was touching so lightly. "And soft," he continued, running the curl between his fingers. "What makes it feel so soft?"

His tone was hushed. Or maybe it was the roar of the falls that made it seem so quiet. Already achingly aware of his presence, she felt his words fall like a transparent silver web around her.

This was a side of him she hadn't suspected. Sensitive, poetic. The fact that he was so terribly male made that quality even more revealing. She was certain that not everyone saw this side of him. And she didn't want to see it, either. It made her waivering resolve so much weaker.

"Creme rinse," she said, swallowing.

A rakish smile deepened the lines bracketing his mouth. His hand trailed over her cheek, his touch feeling like the brush of a butterfly wing. "I suppose your skin looks like honeyed cream because you sleep with a pound of goo on it every night?"

The poet was gone, but the magician remained.

He had to be a magician. The words she'd been preparing to utter stuck where he now touched her throat. The tips of his fingers were moving slowly down, stopping only when they reached the gauzy fabric of her bodice. "Are you this soft all over?"

He was having the strangest effect on her nervous system. It felt very much as if something was about to short-circuit. The prudent thing to do would be to take a step away, but she wasn't so sure she wanted to. It wouldn't hurt to stand here for a minute and find out what he was up to—not that it took a lot of imagination to guess.

It didn't take a whole lot of thought to figure out why her husky, "What do you want?" sounded so breathless, either.

She felt his hand retrace the path up her throat and then anchor itself in the silky hair at her nape. It would have taken only the slightest effort for him to pull her forward, but he did nothing to close the small gap between them.

"I want to know you." An odd thickness deepened his voice. "I want to understand all the things that go on in that beautiful head of yours. What makes you laugh. What you like to do on rainy Sunday afternoons. Why you're always so infuriatingly stubborn... and what it's going to take for you to let me make love to you."

She was held by the intensity in his eyes, and his last words tore at the walls of her rapidly crumbling defenses. If anything, she should be building more barriers, saying something to break the sensuous thread that pulled her to him. But all that passed the constriction in her throat was a whispered, "Why?"

His smile was as gentle as the breeze lifting the leaves off the ancient oaks. "Because you intrigue me. Because I like your independence, yet I can't help wanting to protect you... to possess you. I want to feel you beneath me, to fill you, and make you..."

"Don't!" The word was a broken plea. Heat rushed from the knot in her stomach to where the pulse throbbed frantically at the base of her neck. His words were tormenting her as much as his hands, which had now slid around her back and were holding her against him.

"Don't what, Britt?" His breath, warm against her ear, tangled with the mist of the falls. "Don't answer the question you asked? You always want answers, and I'm quite willing to give them to you." His lips tugged at her earlobe, his tongue tracing its shape and sending wild shocks racing down her spine.

"Creed..."

"Mmmm?" The cool firmness of his mouth left its tantalizing play to explore the arch of her neck.

"Please..." Did she want him to stop? Or was she asking him not to? She didn't know, and Creed didn't allow her time to make a choice.

Shifting against her, he molded her hips to his and claimed her in a slow, agonizing kiss that tore at the very center of her being. The thunder of the falls echoed against the deafening beat of her heart, sound melding with sensation in a swirling vortex of desire unlike anything she'd ever known. His tongue teased hers, its sweet warmth touching the tip of hers then plunging deeply, eliciting a response she was powerless to withhold.

She lifted her arms, her fingers clutching the hard muscles rippling along his back as she sought the support her legs wouldn't offer. Sagging against him made her even more aware of his arousal, heightening her own.

The wildly churning pool below couldn't begin to match the whirl of feelings engulfing her. The rough-tender demands of his tongue had eased to stroke the smooth skin inside her lips. Willingly, she allowed that gentle exploration, just as she allowed his hand to graze her side and move up to cup her breast. His deep, circular motions created waves of heat that shuddered through her. And when his thumb slipped up to tease her hardened nipple, something hot formed there, then shot straight down.

Reality had ceased to exist. There was no past. No future. Only now, and the wonder of surrender she felt in his arms. It was pointless to deny that this was what she'd wanted, for there was something about Creed that had touched the very essence of her spirit.

A ragged moan was drawn from his chest when her fingers caressed the width of his shoulders, her nails raking lightly over his hard flesh. Then, suddenly, he was still.

His one hand left its gentle kneading and locked with his other at the small of her back. "Oh, honey," he rasped, pressing his forehead to hers. "These last couple of days have been absolute hell, and this isn't helping at all."

The way he began stroking her hair was almost soothing. She laid her head against his chest, and could hear his heart pounding as wildly as her own. For several long seconds he simply held her, and Britt made no attempt to move.

"You have no idea how many times I've wanted to haul you out of that damned study just so you'd talk to me." His breathing sounded more even now. "I'd really appreciate it if you wouldn't hide in there anymore. Things are going to get pretty boring if I have to spend all my time alone."

There had been a trace of a smile in his voice, but when he cupped her face and tipped her head back to look down at her, there was no evidence of a smile in his eyes. Only desire. "I want to know you, Britt. All of you. And I want you to know me."

Common sense always had a way of rearing its ugly head. She had to remember who he was—why he was even with her. "Creed," she began, wishing she didn't sound so hesitant. "I really think we should forget about this..."

"Don't tell me to forget what just happened...what *is* happening." His interruption was quiet, his eyes tender. "There's something between us, Britt. You can feel it as well as I can. All we're going to forget are the circumstances that brought us together. Now," he said, planting a kiss on the tip of her nose and taking her by the hand, "let's go get something to eat. There's a great little place on the river that serves terrific steaks—" a teasing grin split his handsome features "—and salads. I'm starving."

Britt had finally met her match. Or was it a kindred spirit? Whichever, it was apparent enough that Creed wasn't going to put up with any arguments. Not, she admitted, that she wanted him to. Rather than rebelling at having lost that precious bit of control, she found herself willingly relinquishing it—and feeling quite content. A hectic, enervating sort of contentment that rivaled anything she'd ever felt before.

That intoxicating feeling burst like an overblown balloon a few hours later. Two police cars were just pulling out of the drive when they returned to the house. A swift, questioning glance at Creed's suddenly shuttered expression told Britt he wasn't surprised to see them there.

Chapter Four

For once, Britt decided she was probably better off not asking what was going on. Creed's ominous silence when he took her key and let them into the house only served to reinforce that decision.

It was almost dusk and the light in the entryway was dim.

"Wait here," Creed ordered, closing the door behind them. He didn't wait to see if she was going to comply before his long strides carried him quickly through the downstairs rooms.

Britt couldn't have moved if she'd wanted to. Shock had rooted her quite firmly to the marble floor.

She was staring into the dining room. The drawers of the huge china closet were open and Mrs. Barnes's exquisite Irish table linens were heaped in a pile on a nearby Hepplewhite chair. The gilt-framed mirror over the antique buffet hung slightly askew and the little Picasso that had been hanging on the wall beside it was gone, as was the alabaster unguent vase that had graced the Spanish oak dining table. Britt had carefully studied the intricate workings on that vase and knew that the early Egyptian artifact was priceless.

It looked very much as if the house had been robbed.

The thought had barely registered when Creed, his expression a study in barely controlled fury, stormed past her and into the study. Within seconds he was on the phone.

"Don't tell me they were in a hurry," she heard him say in a grating voice. "They had the whole damn day and that was no way to conduct a search. You tell them I'm..."

Search? The police had searched the house?

The rest of Creed's increasingly angry words were lost to her. Shock slowly gave way to a sense of betrayal as she turned toward the study.

She had no idea how long she stood there watching Creed. A sense of numbness had seeped through her, giving everything a detached, slow-motion sort of effect. She heard him say something about her thesis. She saw him start pacing in front of the desk. There were books stacked up on the floor. Her eyes wandered to the living room. Two brass candlesticks sat on the hearth. They belonged on the mantle. Creed said something about the money in the safe.

Her eyes and ears were functioning, but her brain couldn't assimilate the information it was being fed. Only one thought was comprehensible. Creed had known about the search.

"I'm sorry about the mess." She turned to find him moving toward her, his eyes steady on her emotionless features. "I'll try to straighten everything up and..."

Her interruption was quiet. "This was why you were in such a hurry to get me out of here this morning, wasn't it?"

She didn't expect a response. The answer was obvious enough. The magic of the afternoon had been only an illusion. The wonderful time they'd spent together meant nothing. It had been just a ploy to keep her away from the house.

"I knew about it," he admitted. Drawing his hand through his hair, he watched her warily. "I thought it would . . ."

"You don't have to explain." Taking an unsteady step toward the stairs, she reached for the dark wood railing. "I understand perfectly."

Creed's irritation was still evident in the tense line of his jaw and his words were sharp. "I suppose you've already made up your mind that you're not going to listen to me?"

Britt took another step up the red carpeted stairs. Her legs felt heavy. "Unless you're going to tell me your men found something that will clear me, I don't want to hear anything you have to say." She didn't even want him to explain why he'd mentioned her thesis while he'd been on the phone. Not now anyway. "I think I've had all the lies I can handle for one day."

The sound of his heavy footsteps coming up behind her provided the impetus she needed to move faster. There was no way she could outrun him, but she was certainly going to try. She'd been too blasted docile today as it was. Not to mention gullible.

She almost made it to her room before his hand clamping around her wrist brought her to a jolting stop. "What do you mean by lies?" he snapped, turning her to face him. There was nothing cool in the blue of his eyes as his gaze bored into hers.

"Let go of me."

"Not until I get an answer."

Tilting her chin in challenge, she glared up at him.

When it became apparent she wasn't going to respond, his grip tightened. "I've never lied to you, Britt." His tone was emphatic, but deadly quiet. "Never."

Her chin inched up further and the tumble of auburn hair fell away from her face. "They say actions speak louder than words." So what if it was a trite phrase? He'd used it on her the other morning and there were times when old truisms couldn't be improved upon. "Your actions have been every bit as deceitful and dishonest as…" An odd constriction had risen in her throat. Swallowing the rest of her words, she freed her hand and stepped away.

She knew now that he'd only pretended to be interested when they'd sat for hours at that quaint riverside restaurant and she'd told him all those dumb stories about her childhood. About how her mother would get so upset when she'd find her in the kitchen peeling potatoes for the cook. How her parents had insisted she take ballet and learn to play the piano. Britt loved ballet, but had thwarted the music lessons by pretending she was tone deaf.

She could discount Creed's feigned amusement at those stories. What she couldn't forget was that he'd probably been just as bored when she'd returned his kisses. His tender seduction, the easy conversation, had only been ways of killing time.

"My actions have been as dishonest as what?"

It was the second time he'd repeated the question and Britt might finally have answered him—except that she'd just turned on the light in her bedroom. Just as her initial shock had turned to a sense of betrayal, betrayal now gave way to an invading sense of violation.

The edge of her bedspread was flipped back as if someone had been looking under the bed for something. The closet doors hung open. The dresser drawers, too. Her room had been searched along with all the others.

"Britt," Creed said from behind her. "Come back downstairs with me."

She wasn't going anywhere with him. "Go away." The command was a broken whisper. "Go away and leave me alone."

The feel of his hands on her shoulders made her stiffen. Whirling around, her dark eyes filled with anger and hurt, she fought to retain her last bit of control. But it was too much. The days of frustration and fear over not being able to prove her innocence and the crazy seesaw of emotions Creed had so carelessly evoked finally broke through that fragile barrier.

"Get out of here!" There was nothing weak about her tone now. "I said leave me alone!"

Creed's jaw clenched, but he didn't move. "There's no way I'm going to leave you alone right now."

"Why not?" she retorted, unmoved by the hurt in his expression. What did he have to look hurt about anyway? "So you can stand there and gloat? You already think I'm guilty even though I keep telling you I'm not. My word doesn't mean anything to you!" She had the feeling she wasn't making much sense, but it didn't matter. "You insist I've committed some crime, so I might as well make your time worthwhile and commit one!"

She grabbed a blue satin throw pillow from the bed and aimed it with commendable accuracy. "Shall I go for assault?" The pillow hit him squarely in the head. "Or how about battery?" She didn't know what the difference between the two was, but she'd seen the term in the newspaper often enough and figured it was as good a crime as any.

A white lace pillow followed the first one. Creed ducked this time and the fluffy bit of fabric slid soundlessly down the wall.

"Maybe you want to get me for bribery?" A circle of blue eyelet hit his knee. "Was that what you were trying to do today?"

She was getting hysterical, but there didn't seem to be a thing she could do about it. There were tears in her eyes and Creed appeared as little more than a huge, dark blur against the pearl-gray wallpaper.

"Maybe you thought if you seduced me, you could turn it around and make it look like I was trying to bribe you with sex! Like you did when you made me kiss you the other morning?" He hadn't made her kiss him, but she wasn't about to give him the benefit of the doubt at the moment.

Another white pillow joined the others.

Creed bent over, picked up the harmless missiles and tossed them back on the bed. She picked one up and promptly threw it back at him, not even noticing that he was replenishing her supply of ammunition.

She was shaking. Her voice was, too. "You didn't mean a thing you said today. All that garbage about wanting us to know each other was just that. Garbage!" Her throat burned with suppressed tears, but her pain egged her on. "You were just buying time to keep me away from here. You could have just said you didn't want me around and I could have spent the day at the library...or you could have locked me in the bathroom!" The blue square she flung this time missed by several feet. "You didn't have to bother with the drive and the falls and the dinner and the walk along the river and..." She ran out of air, along with things to add to her list, and gulped down several ragged breaths.

Taking advantage of the momentary lull in her verbal attack, Creed took a step forward—and raised his arm to ward off another pillow. "I thought it would be easier on you if you weren't around today." He sounded so irritatingly calm. "I didn't think you'd . . ."

Her lungs fortified with a fresh supply of oxygen, she cut him off. "You mean it was easier for you and your men!" She whipped a handful of hair away from her face. "Don't try to make it sound like you were thinking of me when all you were doing was serving your own interests. You don't care how I feel about anything. All you care about is getting your evidence and proving I'm involved in this ridiculous mess!"

He grabbed her wrist just as she backed up to aim another pillow and pushed her hand up against the wall. His other hand flattened on the wall just above her shoulder. "This'd be a helluva lot easier if I didn't care how you feel," he hissed, "and I never said I thought you were guilty."

The tears glistening in her eyes were threatening to spill any moment now and she tried to blink them back. The way he had her pinned, his hand shackling her wrist and his body blocking escape, made her realize how useless her rebellion was. That realization didn't sit well at all. "You never said you thought I was innocent, either."

She couldn't really see his face. Her vision was too clouded with the moisture she was desperately trying to contain. There was nothing wrong with her hearing though. Creed's voice bore an edge that hadn't been there before.

"That's enough, Britt."

"See?" she choked, trying to free her hand from his grip. "You still won't give me a straight answer."

He let go of her wrist. Both of his hands rested on the wall on either side of her head. "That's because you won't believe anything I tell you right now. If I say I believe you, you'll just think I'm trying to placate you." She couldn't argue with that kind of logic. He was absolutely right. "But I'll tell you something you can believe." The harsh edge vanished from his voice and his hands settled on her shoulders. "It's okay to cry." Slowly he pulled her to him. "Cry, honey, and I'll hold you. It'll be all right. I promise."

That's all it took. Britt didn't know if it was his quietly spoken words, or the feel of his strong arms gathering her to him that finally allowed the tears to fall. But they did, with great, gulping sobs.

Creed sank to the side of her bed, drawing her down in his lap. He held her like a small child, cradling her against his chest, stroking her hair. "It'll be all right," he repeated, his breath feathering the curls tumbling over her forehead. "Everything will be all right."

She needed to hear him say that—even if she couldn't quite believe it. The man murmuring those calming assurances was the man who'd unleashed the wild tumult of emotions in the first place, and the last person she should allow to comfort her. She was too upset to bother with that bit of rationalization, though.

She wished she could stop crying. Nothing seemed to stem the flow of tears soaking the edge of his shirt and the hair at the base of his throat. Her hand slid around his back and she clung to the hard muscles there, trying to absorb his quiet strength and regain some semblance of control. There had never been a time in her life when she'd completely given in to her emotions. But, then, there had never been a time in her life quite like this before.

That thought brought a fresh rush of tears cascading down her cheeks.

Creed's hand lay against the side of her head, pressing her to his shoulder. His thumb kept moving back and forth, slowly wiping the moisture from her cheek. Absurdly, the motion reminded her of a windshield wiper blade.

"You're going to drown yourself," he chided, his lips grazing her temple. "Do you want a tissue?"

She shook her head, but he reached over to the nightstand and handed her one anyway. "Blow."

She did, quite inelegantly, and laid her head back down on his chest, weeping even harder. It seemed to take forever before the torrent subsided to muffled, hiccuping sobs. All the while, Creed continued to hold her, soothing her until the sobs faded to more even breathing. She had no idea how long she'd been clinging to him. She only knew she was beginning to feel a little calmer and more rational now.

With the return of her sensibilities came sensations. Where his caresses had been comforting before, they now began to elicit less restful feelings. The heat of his hand stroking the side of her neck was no longer reassuring. The pressure of his fingers trailing lightly over her hip seemed to take on less innocent overtones.

Raising her head, she met his guarded eyes. The thick black lashes surrounding them narrowed as he studied her uneasy expression.

"Are you okay now?" he asked, nudging a curling tendril of damp hair from her cheek.

Nodding, she shifted in his lap. She couldn't get up though. His arms had just tightened and she felt his hand brush against the side of her breast. It almost sounded as if he'd groaned when she moved, but the tight little moan could just as easily have been hers.

Seconds later she was being lifted and set down on the bed. Creed stood in front of her, scanning her tear-stained face while he ran his fingers through his hair. Britt was certain it was just her imagination, but there seemed to be more gray in his sideburns than she'd noticed before. It was quite possible she had a few gray hairs of her own by now.

Thinking about such an inanity was only a feeble attempt at mental diversion. She didn't want to think about how he made her feel, or about how embarrassed she was. Her usual reserve—precarious as it had been lately—had quite clearly disappeared.

Creed jammed his hands into his pockets. "Will you be okay for a few minutes?"

Not able to trust her voice, she just nodded again.

"Get into bed then. I'll be right back." He started to turn, but the widening of her red-rimmed eyes stopped him. "Don't look at me like that," he scolded. "I'm not going to have you 'bribe me with sex' as you so eloquently put it. Making love to you is the last thing on my mind right now."

After all those awful things she'd said to him, his admonition was the least of what she deserved. He didn't have to put up with her tirade. He didn't have to stay with her while she practically dehydrated herself, either. But he didn't have to say he didn't want her!

Why was it that once a person started to cry, even the most inconsequential thing would start the tears up again?

Making love with Britt was hardly the last thing on Creed's mind. The fact that it was uppermost was what had necessitated his sudden departure. All the time she'd been sobbing out her frustration, he'd been dealing with another sort of frustration entirely.

Taking two snifters from the wet bar in the study, he filled them with Scotch. He couldn't find any brandy.

Incredible as it seemed, his hands were shaking.

Creed couldn't understand how, in the space of days, Britt had become so important to him. His physical desire for her was easy enough to explain. He was a normal, healthy male and she was an attractive, and very sexy, woman. No big mystery there. His need to discover everything there was to know about her wasn't so neatly categorized though. That desire had been there since the moment he'd seen her in the interrogation room—and it went far beyond his duty to get information about a suspect in a case. Whatever its basis, he knew it was something he wanted—just as much as he craved the feel of her warm, seductive body.

If he'd kissed her, caressed her the way he'd wanted to while he'd held her on that bed . . .

Muttering an expletive, he shoved the bottle of Scotch back on the shelf. Thinking about making love with Britt was getting him nowhere, so he settled for an equally disturbing thought. It was his fault she'd gotten so upset. If he'd just told her about the search, none of this would be happening now. He could tell she wasn't the type of woman who indulged in frivolous emotional displays. It was clear enough she'd been pushed to the limit tonight, and it must have cost her a lot to let him see her lose the control she held on to with such tenacity.

A wry smile clung to his lips. Just this morning he'd watched her swallow her irritation when he'd ordered her to go for that drive. He'd lost count of the times he'd seen her chin tip at that proud angle and her eyes narrow in silent challenge when he annoyed her. He'd found himself deliberately baiting her just to get that reaction. It was impossible not to admire her control, or her courage.

It was also impossible to overlook the fact that he'd been wrong. His silence had only been meant as protection, but it had been a mistake not to tell her about the search. Even though it wasn't her house, there was something about seeing someone's privacy so thoroughly invaded—no matter how legally—that was psychologically degrading. He had wanted to spare her that.

"Well, McAllister," he muttered, wiping up the drops of liquor he'd spilled on the inlaid wood bar, "are you going to tell her what else is going on around here?" Like the fact that there's a surveillance team outside? he completed to himself.

After what had happened today, he figured she could suspect as much. Maybe he'd talk to her about it in the morning, it might just save him from being flogged with pillows later. She really did have a mean arm.

There was something else going on that Creed wasn't quite so willing to divulge. His detectives had spotted a man watching the house from the forested area behind the property this afternoon. They knew it wasn't Barnes; he and his wife had been traced to Miami. If Creed's intuition was right, his men had seen someone who was a threat to Britt. The danger he posed was very real.

Picking up the snifters, Creed headed up the stairs. He wouldn't talk to her about any of this now. She was upset enough already.

Britt was standing in front of her dresser, tears streaming down her face as she clutched a slip in her hand. There was no sobbing this time. No raggedly drawn breaths. Just tears that refused to stop flowing—over such a little thing, too.

Whoever had gone through her drawers had made an absolute mess of her once neatly folded lingerie.

Creed stood in the doorway, watching while she methodically folded the lacy undergarments and placed them back in the drawer. Except for the dampness on her flushed cheeks and the slightly rigid set of her shoulders, she looked quite calm. A little too calm.

"I do believe you, Britt."

Deep brown eyes turned toward him. There was no disbelief in their shimmering depths. There was no acceptance, either. "You're not just trying to placate me?"

A hesitant smile met the concern in his eyes. "No," he answered simply.

She should have felt relieved. Oddly enough, she merely accepted his words with a barely perceptible nod. She'd had enough emotional upheaval tonight and she couldn't deal with any more feelings. All she felt now was tired and a little numb.

"Here." Creed held out one of the snifters. "Take this and go sit down."

"What is it?"

"Scotch."

Britt rarely drank anything other than wine, and more than two glasses of that were guaranteed to put her to sleep. She accepted the Scotch, though, then dropped to the edge of the bed.

Drawing her hand across her cheek, she wiped away the last of the tears and took a tentative sip of the strong liquid. It tasted terrible. How, she wondered absently, do people ever develop a taste for this stuff?

"If your expression is any indication," Creed said, sitting down next to her, "I'd be inclined to think you're not particularly fond of Scotch."

Her throat still burned. It felt as if she'd just singed her vocal cords. "I think you're . . ." She coughed and tried again. "I think you're safe in assuming that."

"Just think of it as medicine and drink it anyway." He reached over to toy with one of the curls touching her shoulder. "Then I think it would be a good idea for you to get some sleep. Where's your nightgown?" Giving the curl a gentle tug, he watched it spring up to nestle among the others.

At any other time, she would have felt a few distinct twinges of discomfort. It wasn't every day she found herself sitting on a bed drinking with a man who had the disconcerting habit of playing with her hair when he talked to her—and who'd just calmly asked about her nightgown. Right now, though, she didn't have the energy to acknowledge the intimacy of the situation. She felt quite safe. He'd already said he wasn't interested in making love to her.

"There's one in the bathroom." The second swallow of Scotch didn't burn quite so much. After the third one, she decided it didn't taste so bad after all. But it sure did make her feel warm.

Almost as warm as Creed's arm felt when it brushed against hers.

He'd started to get up. Britt's voice stopped him. "What happened to the things that're missing?"

His eyebrows lowered as he settled back. "What things?"

"The artwork. I don't know what all was taken, but there was an original Picasso in the dining room that isn't there now."

"It's all in the recovery room."

An image of the painting lying on a gurney with a sheet pulled over it popped into her head. Next to that stretcher was another with the unguent vase sporting an IV. The mind really did strange things when it was overburdened.

"Some people call it the evidence hold," he clarified. "The stuff was stolen."

"How do you know that?"

"Are you asking me to give away trade secrets?"

His tone was light. Hers was toneless. "No. It's none of my business anyway." It seemed pretty stupid for the Barneses to display stolen art in their house, but that wasn't any of her business, either. "You were talking about my thesis when you were on the phone. I think I have a right to know about that."

Creed's eyes fell to the glass he held suspended between his knees. He seemed to be weighing whatever it was he was going to say. Though he wasn't looking at her, she knew he was also gauging her reaction. "One of the detectives saw it on the desk. He thought the list of paintings you'd compiled might be potential targets for theft." His mouth twisted wryly as he swirled the amber liquid then took an appreciative swallow. "The search squad might not be particularly tidy," he continued, positioning the glass between his knees again, "but you've got to give them points for being thorough."

Britt didn't look as if she was going to give anybody credit for anything.

Creed shrugged. "They'll bring it back first thing in the morning."

Her eyes narrowed. "Bring it back? Where is it?"

"They took it down to the station."

"What?"

"You heard me. I said they'd bring it back in the morning."

"They had no business taking it in the first place." Her declaration wasn't anywhere near as emphatic as it could have been, but at least she was starting to shake off that strange dullness of a few minutes before.

"We had every right to take it." With a look he meant only to be teasing he added, "You'd better hope none of the paintings on that list turn up missing."

She shot him a swift, sharp glance and squared her slender shoulders. "You said you believed me. Was that one of those lies you 'never' told me?"

Taking her glass, he sat it down with his on the night-stand. "I was only kidding," he sighed. "I do believe you. Unfortunately, I'm the only one who does right now. I tried to explain that the list is just part of the work you were doing on your degree, but..." He completed his explanation with a telling shrug and rubbed his jaw. "As for the lies you insist I've told you, I've only lied to you once."

"You said you never had."

"When I said that, I hadn't."

She shook her head, trying to make sense of what he'd just said. There were times when he thoroughly baffled her. "Meaning that . . . ?"

He let the question hang unanswered. Britt grew even more confounded when he grinned, stood up, and disappeared into her bathroom. She couldn't imagine what he was referring to and tried to remember all the things he'd said since they'd come upstairs.

She was still sorting through those fractured bits of dialogue when he returned. Their conversations were immediately forgotten. One minute she'd been staring down at the blue and gray patterns woven into the carpet, and the next she was staring at the denim clinging snugly to his thighs.

"Put this on." He dropped a filmy white gown into her lap. "The Scotch should have relaxed you enough to let you sleep. We'll talk in the morning."

She didn't want to talk in the morning. She wanted to talk now. More than anything else though, she wanted to stop staring at his . . . jeans.

Raising her head, she crossed her arms over the bodice of her sundress and silently congratulated herself for being able to meet his eyes so easily. "I want to know what it was you lied to me about."

"I told you we'd talk in the morning."

"Why do we always have to do things your way?"

"We don't always have to do them my way."

"We do, too. Give me one example of where you've conceded to my wishes."

He mimicked her slightly challenging position by crossing his arms. "You've made it clear you don't want to spend any time with me out by the pool. I haven't tried to press that issue, have I?"

"That's because you know I can't work out there."

"That's just an excuse."

That was true. "We had this discussion already," she returned, refusing to acknowledge the amusement creeping into his eyes.

"Does that mean you don't want to discuss it again?"

She sensed a trap. His expression was far too smug for someone who was about to lose a disagreement. Her responding "Yes" sounded a little wary.

"There's a perfect example then. You don't wish to talk about it, and I concede to your wishes."

"That hardly counts."

"Sure it does." Uncrossing his arms, he bent over and picked up her gown. He didn't straighten though, and his face was only inches from hers. "Are you going to put this thing on, or do I have to undress you and tuck you in myself?"

He was so close she could smell the spicy clean scent of his after-shave. Something about that scent, and his wicked grin, caused her heart to take on a rather unhealthy beat. Scooting back on the bed, she snatched her gown away from him.

Somehow he always managed to work things around so they came out his way, but this was one instance where he wouldn't be so successful. She'd get ready for bed when she wanted to and without his help. "I've never been undressed by a man in my life," she said guilelessly. "And I have no intention of letting you be the first." That statement sounded a little hollow, she thought.

"Oh, come on, Britt." He chuckled and stood up. "You don't expect me to believe..."

He cut himself off, still holding her unblinking glance. As her meaning sunk in, the black slashes of his eyebrows lowered. "Never?"

"You don't have to look like it's a major crime," she mumbled, wishing at the same time she'd just kept her mouth shut. No doubt the status of her virginity would now show up on a police record somewhere. With her luck, they'd probably figure out some way to use it against her. Do they burn virgins at the stake? No, she chided herself. That's witches. In her case, it didn't make a whole lot of difference. Not with the way she'd been acting lately.

She slid back to the edge of the bed, opting for an immediate change of subject. "Why are you in such a hurry for me to go to bed anyway?"

Apparently her revelation had only been of passing interest to him. His expression disclosed very little. "If you could see yourself, you wouldn't ask." Taking her by the arms, he pulled her to her feet. "You look beat. Your eyes are red. That gown has more color than you do. And I don't want you getting sick."

It was pointless to deny that she was tired. She also couldn't deny the languorous warmth seeping through her when his hands ran slowly up her arms and settled on her bare shoulders. The two thin straps of her dress provided no barrier between his light, seductive touch and her cool skin.

Drawing a quiet breath, she tried to focus on the crisp black hairs curling along the edge of his tank-top. It was only the Scotch that was making her feel so warm. The fact that Creed's fingers were now gently massaging the muscles at the back of her neck had nothing to do with it. "I'll go to bed if you'll answer one question for me." What he was doing felt so good.

"That sounds fair."

It was difficult to ignore the way he was stroking her. "What did you lie to me about?"

"Persistent, aren't you?"

"You said you'd answer me."

The gentle motion of his fingers stilled. "I lied about not wanting to make love to you. Are you satisfied now?"

There were times when Britt really wished she hadn't been cursed with this penchant for having to have answers.

"But right now," he whispered, not waiting for the response she couldn't have uttered anyway, "all I'm going to do is kiss you."

Her moan of protest—or was it longing—met the pressure of his lips. She felt his hands drift down her back and he drew her forward, urging her to invite him into the sweetness of her mouth.

It's just the Scotch, she reminded herself when the room seemed to tilt and her hands gripped his shoulders. They felt so solid. As solid as his chest where her breasts were crushing against him.

She knew she was rationalizing. It wasn't the liquor that caused the intense heat coursing through her. She'd felt the same drugging warmth when he'd kissed her before.

His lips brushed lightly against her temple. Lifting his head, he combed his fingers through the silky length of her hair, and smiled. "Creme rinse, huh?"

He dropped a quick kiss on her forehead. A moment later, he'd walked out the door.

It'll be all right. I promise.

Creed's words echoed in her mind while she hurried down the stairs the next morning. Her hair, still wet from her shower, clung damply to the collar of her robe. She always fixed herself a cup of tea and took it back upstairs to drink while she dressed and put on her makeup. The only exception to that routine had been during Creed's first morning here.

The possibility of running into him just yet was remote. Though she hadn't looked out her window to check, she was pretty sure he was at the pool doing his laps at this hour. As soon as she dressed, she'd wait for him to come in so she could apologize for acting like such a jerk last night.

He'd been so patient with her, and in some ways so restrained, that she couldn't help thinking his remark about making love to her wasn't just more of his teasing. She'd been so vulnerable when he'd held her, offering her the security of his arms. If he'd been serious, he could have easily aroused the feelings that just the thought of him seemed to provoke. She'd stayed awake for hours wondering if she would have the strength to resist him—wondering if she even wanted to.

It was a moot point. Creed had done nothing.

Well, she corrected herself, heading toward the kitchen, not exactly nothing. He had said he believed her.

Somehow that made it even harder to deny the feelings she kept telling herself she didn't have.

Britt turned around just as she reached the louvered doors leading to the back of the house. Since she was so engrossed in her thoughts, it had taken a moment for what she'd seen to register. Just to make sure she hadn't imagined it, she walked back to the dining room.

The pile of linens was gone. Pulling open a drawer of the china closet, she found that they'd all been folded and put back. The mirror hanging over the buffet had been straightened, too. In the living room, the brass candlesticks were back on the mantle and the furniture that had been pulled away from the walls was all back in place. Creed must have spent hours cleaning everything up.

Smiling to herself, she started for the kitchen again. As long as she'd be in there anyway, she might as well fix him a pot of coffee.

This time, it was the low, deep tone of Creed's voice that prevented her from reaching her destination.

The double doors of the study were slightly ajar. Moving to them, she could see him leaning against the edge of the desk. His long legs, encased in a pair of faded jeans, were crossed at the ankle and she could see that his feet were bare. The telephone was cradled against his shoulder and his arms were folded over his broad—and naked—chest.

Thoughts of him were always disquieting, the sight of him more so. But what she could hear him saying was even more disturbing, and in a very different way.

"I don't care whose idea it was," he said quietly. "The D.A. isn't going to care, either. She's still an accessory and every bit as guilty."

Britt wasn't sure her heart was even beating when she pushed the doors open and Creed glanced up.

Chapter Five

Britt's slender figure was framed between the open doors. The hem of her foam-green dressing gown brushed the floor and only the tips of her slightly curved fingers peeked from the edges of its flowing sleeves. The darkness of her wet hair accentuated the sudden paleness of her skin and made her unblinking eyes appear even larger than they were. Accusation and fear were barely visible in those guarded depths.

Creed knew what she'd just heard.

He pushed himself away from the desk. Turning from her, he cut his call short and dropped the receiver back on its hook.

There was a certain tension revealed in the corded muscles of his back. When he faced her again, that same tension marked the masculine planes and angles of his face. "It's not what you're thinking." His voice, though quiet, was harsh. His approach deliberate, yet cautious.

"The accessory I was talking about is Henrietta Barnes, not you."

Until it escaped in a soft rush, Britt didn't even realize she'd been holding her breath. All the time she'd been standing there, she'd been telling herself she wouldn't jump to conclusions. Some thread of sense had actually made her listen to that advice, and for that she was grateful. She'd made a big enough fool of herself already without adding a misconstrued conversation to the list.

The list. Her thesis. Maybe asking about that would relieve the odd heaviness that seemed to hang in the air. Why was he glaring at her like that anyway? "Did they bring my papers back yet? I know it's early, but I wanted to work on them in a while."

"A patrolman brought them about an hour ago." Crossing his arms, he directed a sharp nod toward the desk. "A couple of the pages are wrinkled, but I'm sure they're all there."

Britt didn't even look at the stack of papers on the desk. Her eyes were on Creed. He'd turned and was staring at the wall of books on the far side of the room. His eyebrows were lowered in a scowl and his jaw was working. That brooding stance reminded her of a spring that had been wound a little too tight, and she had the distinct feeling her presence was about to send that spring uncoiling.

Obviously she'd encountered him at the wrong time. Aside from the fact that she'd interrupted his call, it was quite possible he was irritated with the way she'd behaved. As it was, she was vacillating between being thoroughly disgusted and downright appalled at the way she'd acted. A little irritation on his part wasn't particularly surprising.

To say he was only a little irritated was somewhat of an understatement. Deciding that deference was the better part of valor—to heck with bravery; she wasn't about to stick around when it looked like it was all he could do to keep from decking someone—she reached for the brass handle on one of the doors.

"I'm sorry for intruding," she apologized, curling her fingers around the latch, "and for being so unreasonable last night." A gracious exit was always preferable to a fumbling one.

His head jerked toward her. It seemed that, until she'd spoken, he'd forgotten she was still there. "Forget it," he muttered. "What are you doing up so early?"

"It's almost eight."

"I was under the impression that eight in the morning was the crack of dawn as far as you're concerned."

There was no teasing in his voice, no betraying amusement lightening his implacable expression. Just the steely coldness of eyes that held no hint of the warmth she'd seen there before.

More wary than ever now, she ignored his curt remark and reached for the handle of the other door. From beneath the crescent of her lowered lashes, she saw his hand fall to his side. His fingers clenched, then relaxed and clenched again. Clearly he was in no mood for conversation, idle or otherwise. An immediate departure was called for.

"Where are you going?"

The left door clicked in its latch. "To the kitchen."

"Do something for me?"

Glancing up just before she pulled the other door toward her, she saw his hand clamp over the back of his neck, and his chest expand with a deep, weary breath. Her eyes got no further than the indentation at the base of his throat before they returned to the triangle of hair curling over that finely honed expanse of flesh. There was something vaguely primitive about the way he was standing there, wearing only those snug denims. She'd admired his physical perfection before—from a purely artistic standpoint, of course. But now that she knew how solid he felt . . .

Giving herself a mental shake, she answered his question with an affirmative nod. There were other things to think about besides the man who looked very much like he wished he'd never laid eyes on her. The only problem was that she couldn't quite remember what those other things were.

"Would you bring me a cup of coffee?" he asked, his fingers working at the knots in his neck. "I put a pot on a while ago, but I got busy and never went back to the kitchen to get it. I need to make some more calls." She stepped back to close the door, but Creed's voice stopped her. "Leave it open. Bring back something for yourself, too. I want to talk to you."

A flicker of apprehension darted through her at his last words. They seemed to contain a threat, and his impersonal manner was making her wonder if he was having second thoughts about believing her.

Her disquiet was more evident than she realized.

"Don't worry." Creed tried to smile, but found that assurance impossible at the moment. "I still believe you."

He shouldn't, but he did—in spite of the fact that his men, whose judgment he both respected and relied upon, were more certain than ever that she knew more than she was telling. If Britt could be convicted on purely circumstantial evidence, she could be put away for the next twenty years.

Creed's next thought, as Britt gave him a faltering smile and walked away, had nothing to do with the others that had been plaguing him for the past two hours. With her hair slicked back, she looked exotic, mysterious. Not the virginal type at all.

Her admission last night had jolted him. The thought that she might be inexperienced had never entered his mind. Though she seemed reserved at times, it was more of an aloof sophistication that had nothing to with timidity. Britt was definitely not shy. Her nature hinted at an I'm-going-to-do-it-my-way attitude that he assumed would include an openness toward sex. Now he wondered if her not having had any intimate relationships regardless of what everybody else did, might be an even stronger statement of her individuality.

There had been no mistaking her physical response to him, though. He had felt the desire in her supple body, tasted the passion she couldn't quite deny.

He wanted her more than ever.

Lowering himself to the chair behind the desk, he propped his elbows on the blotter and covered his face with his hands. Thinking about Britt as a woman instead of a suspect was the last thing he should be doing. The more he thought about her, the less he understood his feelings—and they were definitely bordering on the unprofessional. Why did he feel so strongly that she was innocent when his best men were convinced of her guilt? Those men were certain Britt knew about the man who'd been sighted in the woods again last night—and that she was waiting for an opportunity to give him the money in the safe to take to the Barneses. The only question in their minds was whether or not she would try to escape with him.

Creed couldn't mention that man now. Not if there was a chance Britt did know about him. He valued his integrity above everything else. He would do nothing that might jeopardize the investigation—and pray that his men were wrong.

He was on the phone when Britt returned carrying two mugs. One filled with fragrant herbal tea, and the other with a thick, black liquid that threatened to corrode the heavy ceramic. Creed obviously liked his coffee strong. Since he hadn't had his morning fix of concentrated caffeine, it was no wonder his mood was so awful.

Britt placed his mug in front of him and he nodded toward the leather chairs in front of the desk. Having decided his mood would allow no room for disagreement, she sat down—though she would have preferred getting dressed first. It was one thing to carry on a two-minute conversation with someone while wearing little more than a robe, but this was something else entirely.

Though her dressing gown was less revealing than the dress she'd worn yesterday, there was an implied intimacy in the present situation that her attire—and Creed's lack of it—only accentuated. There was also something very intimate about the way his eyes would wander from her mouth to the outline of her breasts while he cradled the phone against his shoulder and sipped his coffee.

Already uneasy about his attitude, and not willing to allow him to intimidate her further, she decided to return his visual liberties and leveled gratifyingly calm brown eyes at his chest. That little show of impudence earned her the first trace of a smile he'd managed all morning.

When five minutes had passed—four of which Britt had spent staring at the clawed feet of the chair next to her—and Creed was still occupied with his call, she resolved that enough was enough. Why should she sit here listening to him mumble "uh-huh's" and "harrump's" into the phone when she could be upstairs getting dressed?

She pressed her hands into the oxblood leather covering the wide arms of the wing chair and started to rise. The frown accompanying Creed's quick gesture for her to sit back down put a decisive end to that effort, and to his call.

"Sorry," he said, not sounding particularly apologetic as he hung up and pushed his chair back. "I was getting the change of shift report from the surveillance team."

"The surveillance team?"

"That's one of the things I want to talk to you about." Rounding the desk, he stopped in front of her and leaned against it. His movements were as calculated as everything he was about to do. "How do you feel this morning?"

"Fine. Now, what were you saying about a ... ?"

"Did you sleep all right?"

At his interruption, she eyed him narrowly. "You're in no danger of witnessing a performance similar to last night's, if that's what you're getting at."

Her coolly delivered guarantee was met with the slight arch of his eyebrows, but he let her statement pass without comment and continued in the same dry tone. "We're watching the house, Britt. After the way you reacted yesterday, I didn't want you stumbling onto one of my men and then getting upset with me because I hadn't told you they were out there."

That wasn't the only reason he was telling her this. If she was involved with the Barneses, his presence here would have given her reason enough to suspect additional surveillance. Having that suspicion confirmed might press her into carelessness. No matter what his men thought, she wasn't sophisticated enough to avoid panic. If she wasn't involved, his advice wouldn't make any difference.

Though his flinty blue eyes revealed nothing, Britt knew he was measuring her reaction. She was more concerned with his coolness than with what he'd just said. So what if the police were watching the place? They'd already tapped the phone lines.

"Do you want me on my knees, Creed?"

Her response threw him. "What?"

"I appreciate your telling me about your men, but I can assure you that if I'd run into one of them, I wouldn't 'get upset' again. I've already said I'm sorry about what happened last night and I refuse to grovel to get you to accept my apology. The search just caught me off guard and, from now on, I promise I won't be surprised at anything else that happens around here. Now, if there's nothing else..."

"Sit down," he ordered when she started to stand. "We're not through yet."

Britt shrank back in the chair, her eyes fixed on the imposing figure looming over her. The man staring at her now bore no resemblance whatsoever to the man she'd come to know. There was a threatening glimmer of warning in his unrelenting expression, and indomitable authority in his stance. She had never seen anyone look quite so... hard.

What she didn't realize was that Creed was forcing himself to separate his unnamed feelings for her from the need to discover if there was something she was hiding. That dichotomy was possible only by acknowledging that she was a suspected felon. Even still, he wasn't so sure he was succeeding.

He needn't have worried. There was nothing in his manner to betray any of his finer emotions when he started questioning her. To Britt, it was the scene in the interrogation room all over again, only worse. Creed's terse questions made the other officer's inquiries seem like polite proddings. At least that officer had managed to smile once in a while.

When Creed abandoned the desk to start pacing over the richly patterned rug, his eyes never leaving her face while she responded to his questions, Britt decided he'd missed his calling. He should have been a prosecuting attorney. He had a definite knack for badgering the witness.

For over an hour, she alternated between confusion and suppressed anger as she answered him, always in the same certain voice. *Yes*, Mr. Barnes told her how much to collect from his "customers." *Yes*, they always gave her cash.

"Don't you think that's odd? Don't art dealers take checks, or deal on letters of credit?"

It wasn't her place to question the method of payment, and she told him so. And, *Yes*, she always counted the money before she put it in the safe. *No*, there hadn't been five deliveries. There had been only three. *No*, the Barneses hadn't made any arrangement for her to deliver the money to them. *Yes*, she was sure! *No*, there was no one else involved that she knew of.

Then she answered the same questions all over again.

Britt hated having to repeat herself, and the feelings she had toward the man who regarded her with such cold indifference were leaning in the same direction. How could she possibly have thought she cared for him when he so obviously cared nothing about her? It didn't seem to matter to him that she was the same woman he'd held last night. The same woman he'd hypnotized with his tender words at the falls. Even the promise he'd made didn't matter. He'd promised that everything would be all right. But everything was all wrong.

The old grandfather clock standing guard in the entry struck the half hour. Its low, reverberating bong punctuated the tense silence that had filled the study for the last several seconds.

Creed was standing by the windows behind the desk, staring out at the broad expanse of lawn edging the circular drive. It was impossible to tell whom this had been harder on—him or her. It had been worth it, he decided, because now he was certain she was telling him everything she knew, which was next to nothing. But because his men thought otherwise, he couldn't disregard their theory and tell her about the man who might be out there even now.

Creed had an idea of his own, however, one he would soon discuss with his detectives. Since Britt knew the combination to the safe, that man might need her to get it—or he might try to use her for a hostage to insure safety for himself and the Barneses.

Cupping his hand over his neck, he expelled a heavy breath. Neither theory could be proven until that man made a move. All Creed could do now was try to protect Britt without her knowing about it. Some vacation, he thought.

Not knowing if he was finished, or if he was just taking a minute to regroup before launching another attack, Britt slid to the edge of her chair. "I've told you the truth," she said, raking her fingers through the curls of her now-dry hair. "*All* of it."

"I know."

"Then what was the inquisition for?"

"Assurance," was his quiet reply.

Exasperation turned to bewilderment when he turned and she saw his penitent smile. She'd once thought of him as a chameleon. Now she wondered if Jekyll and Hyde might not be a more accurate comparison.

"I needed to assure myself I was right about you," he clarified. Jamming his hands into his pockets, he leaned against the edge of the desk again. "It's not easy being a majority of one."

"If you're referring to your being the only one who believes me, then you can double that majority. I believe me, too."

She didn't want to sound so defensive, but she didn't have Creed's ability to dissemble so rapidly. The best she could do was crawl behind the wall of her practiced reserve and hope none of what she was feeling would show through the cracks. She wasn't too sure what she felt at the moment anyway—other than that she wasn't particularly crazy about him right now.

"I hope this little exercise has finally put your mind at ease," she continued, annoyed with the smile in his eyes. "I know I've found it extremely enlightening."

"Would you care to explain that remark?"

"Not particularly."

"Do it anyway."

"Is that an order... Captain?"

Immediately she regretted her sarcasm. Just because he kept putting her through an emotional wringer didn't mean she had to lower herself to such uncivilized behavior. After all, he was only doing his job.

"No, Britt," he sighed, looking wounded. "It wasn't an order. I can only imagine what you found enlightening about being treated like a..."

"A common criminal?" she offered quietly.

"Or worse. I'm sorry, but this isn't easy for me, either."

"What's so difficult about it for you? This is what you do every day, isn't it?"

"Hardly."

"You mean you don't spend all your time trying to catch the bad guy?"

He got that indulgent look. "That's not what I'm talking about."

Her voice grew quieter still. "The position you're in with your men, is that it?" How could she stay angry with him when he chose to believe her and no one else did?

"It isn't uncommon for a team to disagree about motive or suspects. Different opinions help us cover more possibilities. I can handle that."

"Then what do you mean? What is it about this that you're finding so difficult?" And why, she added to herself, can't you ever give me a straight answer?

The answer she got couldn't have been more explicit. She didn't see the soft light in his eyes when he glanced away though. All she caught was his terse, "You."

She knew it. He was still irritated with her.

Looking down at her lap, she twisted the belt of her robe around her finger. "We don't exactly bring out the best in each other, do we?"

She didn't look up from the coil she was winding, but she didn't miss his wry smile. It was there in his voice. "I think that's a fair statement to make at the moment, although there have been a few times when what we brought out in each other was quite . . . pleasant."

It was hard to ignore the implication behind his words—and the corresponding leap of her pulse—but she managed. Verbally, anyway. "So—" letting go of the tight ball of green silk, she watched it unravel ''—now that you've got the phone bugged and your crew is watching the place, what are we supposed to do?''

''We haven't *bugged* the phone,'' he replied, amused. ''A tracer's been put on it. And it's a team, not a crew. As for you and me, we just do what we've been doing. We wait...and try to make the best of a difficult situation.''

Which situation was he referring to? There were two very distinct ones as far as Britt was concerned. The obvious one—the one he was probably talking about—was this mess with the Barneses. But the one that was even more ''difficult'' was Creed's presence. How could she make the best of that?

All kinds of possibilities raced through her mind, every one of which she hastily banished as she drew herself to her feet. ''I'd better go get dressed.''

Slipping between the chairs, she headed for the double doors.

In physical reinforcement of the course he knew he had to take, Creed's hands curled into fists inside his pockets. For now, he would keep his hands off of Britt. Professionally, he had no choice. Emotions were dangerous; he'd seen too many mistakes made by men whose feelings had overridden their logic. But he didn't want to risk losing ground with her, either. ''Britt?'' he called just as she reached the banister. ''Would you do something for me?''

Giving him a sideways glance, she shrugged. ''Sure.'' He probably wanted more coffee.

On the other hand, maybe he wanted something else. The devilish smile in his eyes when he motioned for her to follow him into the kitchen caused her to wish she hadn't acquiesced so readily. That smile made her nervous.

Keeping his hands off Britt didn't include non-sensual types of contact, he rationalized, and when she came through the door, he grabbed her by the elbow. Just as he expected, she immediately responded with a scowl, "What are you doing?"

"You said you'd do something for me," he reminded, not letting go of her arm until they were standing in front of the sink.

"Yes, but . . ."

"You can't do it anywhere except here."

She was almost afraid to ask what "it" was. The last time they'd stood in front of the sink—the morning she'd burned her hand—he'd kissed her. Rather, she'd kissed him. Was that what he was up to again?

Tipping her head back so she could see something other than his chest, she dryly inquired, "Just what do you have in mind?"

His lazy gaze fell to the soft part of her lips. There was an invitation there he was finding extremely difficult to ignore. It seemed like some sort of perverted justice that she might be lowering her guard just when he'd decided on the hands-off approach.

"Breakfast," he returned with a grin.

"Breakfast?" The disappointment in her tone was quickly covered with incredulity. "You want me to fix you breakfast?"

"You don't have to make it sound like I asked you to prepare a meal for the third fleet. All I want is an omelet like the one you made the other morning." His hands found his pockets again. That seemed to be the only place he could put them to insure they wouldn't somehow wind up on her shoulders, cupping her face, or tangling in her hair. She had beautiful hair. "If you don't want to make it for me, just tell me how you did it and I'll make it myself. You can supervise."

That smile of his was totally disarming, and Britt was tempted to give in. This was the man she'd shared the quiet conversation with yesterday. The one who had kindled the strange warmth that had never really left her. Something about him made her feel safe, protected. Maybe that was why she'd never quite grasped the reality of what would happen to her if she couldn't prove her innocence.

Shoving those thoughts aside, she reminded herself that he was also the same man who'd raked her over the proverbial coals less than ten minutes ago. "Fix me a cup of tea and I'll tell you how to make it."

"Fix your own tea."

"Do you want to know how to make the omelet?"

"Do you want to be arrested for insubordination?"

It wasn't what he'd said. It was the realization that she was actually teasing him that made her back down a bit. "If you'll fix my tea, I'll fix your breakfast."

"I don't believe it." Creed's hands came out of his pockets and he crossed his arms.

Being eye level with that beautifully molded chest and seeing the muscles flex with his movement almost made her forget the question she wanted to ask. "Ah...what don't you believe?"

"I'm not sure...but I think we just compromised."

"Don't push it, McAllister," she mumbled, wishing he'd go put on a shirt. Did he always run around half-naked? "You just have more ammunition than I do."

"I didn't realize we were at war."

At his suddenly serious tone, she raised her eyes to his. He just smiled, and turned to put the teakettle on the burner.

It wasn't so much a war as it was a battle of wills. The only problem was that Britt had the feeling that if she won, she might lose. In some vague, convoluted way that made sense to her, but she had no idea of what Creed's definition of victory might be.

She wasn't going to ask, either.

Reaching up to take one of the copper pans from the rack above the center island, she glanced backward over her shoulder. "I suppose you want bacon?"

Creed was leaning against the counter next to where he'd placed a clean mug. "I'll fix the bacon. Wouldn't want to risk ruining our truce by offending your sensibilities."

"Oh, knock it off, Creed." She opened the refrigerator and, arms filled with eggs, cheese, butter and bacon, she kicked the door closed. "Just because I don't eat it, doesn't mean I can't cook it. Here—" depositing those ingredients on the counter, she reached into the bin beneath the sink and tossed him an onion "—make yourself useful."

"What am I supposed to do with this?"

She thought he was serious, at least until she glanced up to find him grinning at her again. He wasn't looking at her face, though. She was still bent down in front of the sink and the slit of her robe had fallen open to reveal a generous amount of shapely calf and thigh. "I don't think you want me to answer that," she advised sweetly, and gave the belt of her robe a tug as she rose.

His eyes were on the silky green fabric that now covered what he'd seen a moment ago. Slowly they made their way over the curve of her hip, across her flat stomach, and up to settle on the feminine contours of her chest. Though she was literally covered from neck to toes, she felt as if her robe had vaporized beneath his searing inspection.

Curling her fingers around the button at the base of her throat, she turned away. He hadn't touched her, but his visual caress had left her just as shaken.

"Chopped or sliced?"

"What?" She grabbed three eggs and started cracking them into a bowl.

"The onion. How do you want it?"

"Chopped."

Silence ensued as each concentrated on their separate tasks. At least Creed tried to concentrate on what he was doing. He'd much rather be peeling that robe off Britt than peeling the skin off an onion, and he was beginning to wonder why he'd made that stupid resolution to keep his hands to himself.

The heavy knife he held was moving rhythmically over the cutting board when he slanted a glance to where Britt stood at the stove. Her back was to him and she was reaching up to take another skillet from the overhead rack. His eyes narrowed when they fixed on the firm roundness of her bottom and he tried to visualize the smooth expanse of thigh he'd seen before. The knife missed the onion, but not his finger.

Britt was wiping her hands on a towel and trying not to think about how domestic everything seemed at the moment when she turned to find Creed standing behind her.

"I'll watch the legs ... er, the eggs, if you'll go get me some tape."

"What did you ... ?" Seeing the droll twist to his mouth, and it being quite apparent what he'd done—a paper towel was wrapped around the index finger of his left hand and there was a fair amount of crimson soaking through it—she stifled the unnecessary question and scooted past him. The half bath by the back door seemed like a logical place for the Barneses to keep first-aid supplies.

"I don't need that," Creed informed her when she returned. The disclaimer was directed at the bottle of antiseptic she was holding. "Just give me the tape."

She handed him an adhesive strip, then watched him try to rip open the wrapper with his teeth while he held the paper towel around his finger. "Oh, give me that." It took a great deal of effort not to smile as she snatched the strip of flesh colored plastic from between his teeth. "Go wash your finger off."

He didn't move.

Remembering the way he'd treated her when she'd burned her hand, and figuring that turnabout was fair play, she stepped behind him. Flattening her hands on his back, she pushed him to the sink. It was a little like moving a block of granite. "Give me your hand."

When he didn't comply, she reached over and grabbed his wrist. "Hold still," she admonished, keeping her head bent so he couldn't see the laughter she was trying to suppress. He was acting like a recalcitrant little boy, but that was only part of the reason for her smile. The way his muscles flexed and the sharp intake of breath when she pressed against his arm to anchor it told her he wasn't immune to her touch. There was something very satisfying about that.

Just as there was something very dissatisfying about his failure to take advantage of their proximity. He could have easily pulled away. He could just as easily have closed the tiny gap between them. He did neither. All he did was stand there, tensely allowing her to clean the small cut. Maybe she should press him back against the counter like he'd done to her and . . .

Creed's low growl cut through her audacious thoughts. "I don't want that stuff."

Grateful that her mental wanderings had been interrupted, she uncapped the bottle of orangy-red liquid. "Don't be a baby," she chided. "It'll only sting a little."

"It stings a lot and I don't want it."

The light of laughter in her eyes met the stubborn resolve in his. This big man—this big, tough cop—was afraid of a little sting? "It won't hurt that much. You need something on it so it doesn't get infected."

"It's not going to get infected."

Impulse goaded by a tiny thread of teasing perversity dictated her actions. "Since you seem so sure of that, then I guess you won't need this, either." Folding the adhesive strip in her palm, she slipped past him, calling over her shoulder as she left the kitchen, "Sauté the onions before you put them in with the eggs."

Her hand hit the rail of the curving staircase and she almost made it to the second step. Creed's grip on the back of her belt made any further progress impossible. As the thin cord dug into her stomach, some little voice inside her head asked what had taken him so long.

Only her hold on the railing kept her from falling against him when he gave her belt a tug from behind. "Give it to me."

"Give you what?" she returned with feigned innocence.

"Britt."

If he was trying to sound firm, he was failing miserably.

The underlying chuckle in his voice became an ill-disguised smile when she turned around. He didn't let go of her belt, though, which meant that his arm was now around her waist. And, since she was standing on the bottom step, she could also see over his shoulder. She was facing the front door.

The way her body stiffened had nothing to do with the way Creed's palm had flattened at the base of her spine. Her tight moan when she closed her eyes bore no relation to the loss she felt when he jerked back and spun around to see what had caused her color to disappear.

The force behind his demand made his voice harsh. "Who's that?"

It couldn't be. The fates wouldn't do this to her. A split second later, Britt opened her eyes. Sure enough, the woman was still there, staring at them through the beveled glass window of the door. "Oh, Mother," she all but groaned. "Why now?"

Chapter Six

Creed looked anything but pleased. Grasping Britt's arm he coaxed her down from the step. "Let her in," he directed impatiently, "and for God's sake, smile."

He stayed where he was, his mind racing while he watched Britt, looking as if she was on her way to the gallows, pull open the door.

The woman wrapping Britt in a tight hug could only be described as striking. Though her auburn hair was generously sprinkled with silver, she wore her age as well as she did her designer suit and matching beige shoes. Everything about her spoke of cultured breeding—including the very proper scowl being directed over her daughter's shoulder.

Creed dipped his head in a greeting that wasn't even acknowledged by those sharp hazel eyes when he crossed the entry. He didn't bother feeling slighted. He was too busy trying not to groan when he saw the luggage the cabbie was depositing at the front door. This was all he needed right now.

Ordinarily, Britt would have been delighted to see her mother, but that was the last thing she was feeling. Helen Chandler was a born worrier and there was enough going on here to give her an ulcer and keep it active for months.

Britt tried to smile when she stepped back. "What are you doing here, Mom?"

"Coming to see you, of course. I tried to call you yesterday..." Helen stepped farther into the entry, all but ignoring Creed who'd just set her luggage inside before he'd closed the door. "...and your line was busy when I tried again from the airport a while ago. Your father's in Hawaii and I thought I'd stop off to see you before I joined him."

Her mother's tone was a bit more clipped than usual. Not surprising under the circumstances, Britt supposed. Dressed only in her robe with her hair a riot of tangled curls, it certainly must look as if she'd just crawled out of bed. Creed's lack of attire—not to mention the way he'd been holding her at the foot of the stairs—probably made it look as if he'd been in bed with her. Imagining the worst of what her mother might think was a habit Britt had developed a long time ago.

Brushing an invisible speck of lint from her linen jacket, Helen turned to Creed. "I don't believe I've had the pleasure."

Britt blanched at the thread of disapproval woven through her mother's graciousness. At the moment, she would have given anything to have a hole open conveniently beneath her feet. How was she ever going to explain Creed's presence? She couldn't tell her mother why he was here!

Explanations were something she didn't have to worry about. The silencing glance Creed shot her indicated he had everything under control.

Sliding his arm around Britt's shoulder, he bestowed a charming smile on her mother and extended his free hand. "The pleasure is mine, Mrs. Chandler." He took Helen's hand and, in a surprisingly European gesture, brought the back of it to his lips. "I'm Creed McAllister... Britt's fiancé."

When he'd put his arm around her seconds ago, Britt had thought the gesture almost protective. The way his fingers were biting into her upper arm now brought the real reason for that gesture into focus. He was warning her to keep her mouth shut.

Figuratively, she did. Literally, it was hanging open.

"Brittany?" The inflection of Helen's tone seemed to ask no less than a dozen questions. The ones immediately coming to Britt's mind were, What on earth is going on? Who is this man? And, Have you lost your mind? The only one she heard was, "Why didn't you tell us?"

"It... it was a bit sudden," Britt offered weakly, and the pressure on her upper arm decreased perceptibly.

Creed looked back at Helen. "I was just about to have breakfast. Why don't you join me while Britt dresses?"

To Britt's way of thinking, her mother didn't look anywhere near as skeptical as she should have. "That's a lovely idea, Creed. I had breakfast on the plane, but a cup of coffee would be nice... if you have any. I know Brittany doesn't drink it."

He chuckled and gave Britt a tiny nudge toward the stairs. "She hasn't converted me yet." Placing his hand in the small of Helen's back to escort her away, he glanced back at Britt. "Bring a shirt for me when you come down, will you, honey?"

Either he didn't see the sparks flashing from Britt's eyes, or he chose to ignore them as he edged Helen into the kitchen.

Britt was numb. Britt was relieved. Britt was furious! And she didn't want to leave Creed alone with her mother a second longer than was absolutely necessary.

There was nothing ladylike about the way she took the stairs two at a time and tore into her bedroom. Not only did she have to contend with the prospect of jail, now she was faced with her very straitlaced mother—and a resident cop who'd just become her "fiancé"!

Why is it, she wondered, that just when you think things can't possibly get worse, they invariably do?

Fury had given way to an equally strong surge of reasonableness by the time she'd scrambled into her navy blue roll-sleeved blouse and casual white skirt. In less than ten minutes, she'd managed to dress, swipe mascara over her lashes, and tame her mahogany waves with the navy-and-red striped scarf she'd tied at the nape of her neck.

Donning an expression of what she hoped was composure, but probably resembled something more like controlled panic, she curbed her harried pace and headed into the kitchen.

Creed was sitting at the table in the breakfast nook, just finishing his breakfast. Helen occupied the chair across from him, casually sipping her coffee while talking about how much she and Britt's father had enjoyed their trip to Switzerland last year. Apparently she'd already wormed Creed's background out of him and knew that his father was an ambassador there. Leave it to her mother to waste no time probing the roots of his family tree.

"Can I get you more coffee, Mom?" Britt's smile faltered a little when she met the warning in Creed's eyes. He didn't have to bother with that. She wasn't about to do anything to arouse her mother's suspicions.

"Thank you, dear, but I'm fine for now."

Britt acknowledged her with a nod, then turned to Creed. "Here's your shirt." She held out the light blue cotton T-shirt she'd found draped over his doorknob and wondered if she shouldn't have added "honey" to her statement. Being reasonable meant going along with this little hoax until she could figure out what other alternatives she had—but there was no sense going overboard.

"Thanks...honey," he said with a grin, taking the shirt and his empty plate and moving to the sink. "Do you want your tea now? It's ready."

She watched his head disappear beneath the blue cotton, then emerge a second later. "Please," she returned. What she really wanted was another shot of the Scotch he'd given her last night.

"Are you all right?" Helen inquired as Britt sank into one of the empty chairs. "You look rather pale."

Britt opened her mouth, but Creed's words answered. "I've been trying to get her to lay out by the pool—" his hand cupped her shoulder as he placed a mug of tepid tea in front of her and she felt his fingers slipping beneath her hair "—but she insists on spending all day cooped up in the study working. A little sun would do her good, don't you think?"

Britt had the feeling she was being manipulated somehow, but the way his fingers were massaging the tense cords in her neck was making it difficult to concentrate on anything other than trying to act normal. What was normal behavior for a woman who'd just become engaged to her warden anyway?

"I'm sure you've discovered that Brittany can be quite stubborn at times."

"It's an inherited trait," Britt returned in the same affectionate tone her mother had used. "I get it from her."

When he gave her shoulder a squeeze and moved back to his chair, it was all Britt could do to keep from sighing her relief. It was too hard to think when he was touching her.

"So, how long will you be staying, Mom?" Please, she begged silently, please tell me you're only laying over for a few hours.

"I'd thought I'd just spend the night, but now that I've got a wedding to plan..." A smile completed her sentence.

"Oh, you don't have to plan anything!" The panic in her voice earned her a sharp kick in the shin from under the table. "I mean, we aren't... That is, we haven't..."

"We haven't had a chance to discuss what we want yet," Creed supplied smoothly, raising his mug to his lips.

Helen looked worried. "You're not going to elope, are you?"

"Definitely not." Britt's tone was so emphatic that her mother couldn't help being mollified. "I promise we won't elope."

Creed smiled into his cup.

"Well—" Helen tapped a manicured nail thoughtfully on her chin "—let's see. There are so many people we would want to invite. You *are* planning on having the wedding in Boston, aren't you?"

"It'll be in Boston," Britt assured, thinking that it would be, if she ever had a wedding. "Since no date's been set, I think it's all a little premature to talk about right now. Would you like to see the house? Mrs. Barnes has a collection of Eisenglass I'm sure you'd like, and the grounds are quite . . ."

Helen patted her daughter's arm, the motion interrupting the glaring attempt to change the subject. "I'm sure the grounds are lovely, and I'll take a look at the collection later. If you have something else you'd rather do, go ahead. I'll just sit here and visit with my future son-in-law." She turned back to Creed who was looking maddeningly nonplussed by all of this.

Britt received her mother's message loud and clear. A few minutes ago, she couldn't have imagined anything more disastrous than leaving Creed and her mom alone. Now, she couldn't think of anything more fitting. He clearly wasn't going to say anything about what was really going on, and it would serve him right to undergo the interrogation her mother was dying to subject him to.

"Well, there are a few things I'd like to take care of. So, if you don't mind . . ." With an elegant shrug, she started past Creed.

His hand snagged hers, his expression quite unremarkable considering the fact that he was cutting off the circulation in her fingers. "I'm sure whatever you have to do can wait for a while. Stay with us."

That smile of his didn't fool her for a minute. He was giving her an order.

With a feline curve to her lips, she unobtrusively pushed her coral-tinted thumbnail against his wrist. His grip immediately slackened. "I think you two can get to know each other better without me around," she purred. Playing her role to the hilt, she stroked back the curly black hair tumbling over his forehead. For once, she was going to do something her way. "I'll be in the study."

If her mother saw the way his jaw clenched, nothing in her satisfied smile betrayed it. "I'll get us some more coffee," she told Creed as Britt strolled out of the kitchen.

Any satisfaction Britt felt over having won that minor skirmish vanished about an hour later. Creed, looking relatively unscathed, crossed the study, slapped his palms down on the desk, and leaned over the papers she'd strewn over the top of it. "Your mother's waiting for you in the living room, so you'd better get in there." The agitation in his tone when he brought his face to within inches of hers made his voice a furious whisper. "Don't you ever pull another stunt like that again, Britt. The next time I tell you I want you to stay, you stay. Understand?"

Britt was forced to reevaluate her initial opinion. Obviously he hadn't come through her mother's inquisition quite so well after all. She kept her voice low, though her mother couldn't possibly have heard them. "What's the matter, Creed? Don't you like the role you've elected to play?"

She'd never really understood the phrase "if looks could kill." Not until now, anyway. "My personal preferences don't have anything to do with this. You're supposed to cooperate and that means . . ."

The sharp summons of the phone ended his terse reprimand. It also momentarily ended their opposition. For one heart-stopping second their eyes locked in mutual trepidation.

More likely than not, the call would be for Creed. But what if it was Mr. Barnes? How would they handle that with her mother around?

Creed drew back. "Answer it."

She did. The relief in her eyes told Creed that the call was for him even before she handed him the receiver.

Cupping his hand over the mouthpiece, he growled, "Don't say anything stupid," and turned his back to the challenge in her eyes.

Britt would have slammed the door if her mother hadn't been in the next room. As it was, she just closed it quietly and resigned herself to the fact that it was going to be a while before she could tell him what she thought of the new mess he'd gotten her into. In the meantime, she'd just have to try to get herself out of it the best she could.

Certain that her mother had uncovered a few major flaws in his background, if not his character, she started confidently for the living room. Her mother would hardly press for a wedding date if she was trying to talk her out of marrying him.

Things were starting to look up. At least she thought so for about six seconds. Her mother's smile was stretched from one eighteen-karat gold earring to the other. Britt's heart sank before her mother even opened her mouth. "He's perfect for you, Brittany. I can't wait to tell your father."

Naturally, Creed's call didn't take long. Within minutes, Helen, refusing to be sidetracked by Britt's attempts to interest her in Eisenglass, Stubenglass and anything else she could think of, was talking to the overseas operator.

Whether Creed's grip on her hand was to give assurance or seek it, Britt didn't know. All she knew for certain was that her mother was gushing Creed's praises to her father and moments later Britt was receiving her father's lovingly gruff blessing. If Creed hadn't realized the impact of what he'd done before, he surely must have by the time he'd been welcomed into the family by Mr. Chandler.

It wasn't until Helen went upstairs to rest before dinner that Britt had any hope of cornering Creed alone. He must have known what was coming, though. The minute Helen hit the top landing he mumbled something about having to make a call and closed himself in the study.

Glaring at the closed doors, Britt decided to give him five minutes. If he wasn't off the phone by then, she'd barge in there. To heck with his rules. He didn't deserve to have them obeyed anyway. Not only had he charmed the silk stockings off her mother, but he'd been enjoying his new role far too much.

"Put your arm around me," he'd whispered when the three of them had taken a walk through the formal gardens, "and stop stiffening up every time I touch you. We're supposed to be engaged, remember?"

Terribly conscious of her mother several yards away admiring the roses, she'd slipped her arm around his waist. The wistful smile that had come to Helen's face made Britt angrier than ever with Creed. Obviously their murmurings were being mistaken for tender endearments and Britt hated the thought of deceiving her mother this way.

She kept her voice low and gazed up at him with an expression of rapt adoration. "I'll get you for this, McAllister."

The gentle kiss he brushed to her forehead quelled some of her indignation—until she reminded herself it was just part of the act. His eyes held nothing—except challenge. "Do you honestly think you're in a position to issue threats?" he'd taunted.

Remembering his smug expression, and how powerless she'd felt at that moment, she decided that five minutes was more of a reprieve than he deserved. He'd put her off long enough.

Creed wasn't on the phone. He was standing in front of the window nursing a drink. Not bothering to turn around when she stepped into the study and closed the door, he acknowledged her with a flat, "I poured you a drink. It's on the bar."

The very least she'd expected was some guilty defensiveness on his part. He didn't come across that way at all. If anything, he sounded a little put out. The fact that he seemed more interested in the shrubs outside the window than in her presence was also pretty annoying.

Ignoring the glass he'd filled for her, she fixed a withering glance on the back of his head. If he thought she was going to waste time with preliminaries, he was sadly mistaken. "I realize you didn't want me to blow your cover, but wasn't telling my mother we're engaged a little drastic?"

His shoulder lifted in a dismissive shrug. "After everything you'd told me about your parents, I didn't think you'd want it to look like you were just shacking up with somebody. Since I have to stay here, it was the only thing I could come up with on such short notice. Besides—" he turned and leaned against the windowsill "—you've adapted quite well. Telling her I'm staying here while my apartment's being painted was a nice touch."

The glass he held was raised in an absent salute. Britt's nails bit into her palms. It was not only aggravating, it was totally unfair that he should be able to switch masks so rapidly. He'd played his chosen role to perfection all day. Now that he didn't have to keep up that pretext, he couldn't have looked more bored.

"Just because you told her we're engaged isn't any excuse for you to stay here. I had to come up with something to make this...this 'arrangement' sound plausible."

"And aboveboard?" he queried dryly.

"And aboveboard," she agreed, peeved.

"I hardly had time to think out all the details, Britt. You're not the only one who finds this situation distasteful, you know."

Her aggravation wouldn't let her acknowledge the dull pang his unflattering remark brought. Was that how he felt about playing the part of her fiancé? "I suppose 'distasteful' is one way of describing the mess you've gotten me into."

"You're not the only one in it . . . and keep your voice down, will you? Your mother's room is right above us and I don't want it to sound like we're arguing."

"We *are* arguing!" Britt's voice was quieter, but quite emphatic.

"No, we're not. If you want to talk about this, we'll *discuss* it. Look at it this way, things could be worse."

After having spent most of the day with him at her side, his little caresses—no matter that they were all for show—adding a heady note of intimacy to the otherwise general conversations, it seemed a little strange that there was so much space separating them now.

Britt walked over to the bar, not to get any closer to him, but to get the drink still waiting for her. "I can't imagine how things could possibly be worse," she muttered, then took a tentative taste of the strong liquor. Reminding herself it would taste better after the third swallow, she took another.

"Oh, they could be." Creed's wry chuckle ended with a generous gulp of his own Scotch. "I could have told her we were married. At least this way, you don't have to share your bed with me tonight. I doubt she'd accept the idea of separate bedrooms for newlyweds."

Britt wasn't sure, but she could have sworn he was smiling when he turned and dropped into the obscurity of one of the wing chairs in front of the desk. Now, only the top of his head was visible over the high red leather back.

Since he couldn't see how well she was handling his last remark, she took her glass and leaned against the desk in front of him. His elbows were propped up on the arms of the chair and he was studying the glass he held steepled in his hands. "For your sake," she advised nonchalantly, "it's a good thing you didn't. You wouldn't have gotten much sleep."

The first real expression she'd seen since she'd come in here finally registered on his face. His brows snapped together and his gray-blue eyes seared a path from her waist to her neck before locking on her eyes. "I wasn't implying that we would have done anything other than *share* a bed."

That hurt. "I was implying even less," she returned, smoothing her skirt. "You wouldn't have shared my bed. You would have slept in the bathtub." He wasn't the only one who could deliver not-so-subtle put-downs. "But there's no point in discussing a hypothetical situation, so we might as well get this over with. What are we going to do about my mom?"

"You tell me." He looked positively brooding. "She's your mother."

"True. But this was all *your* brilliant idea."

"Don't remind me."

"I really wish you'd stop sounding like that. How do you expect me to play the part of loving fiancée when you're acting like you'd rather be having all your teeth pulled without novocaine?''

"How in the hell do you expect me to act right now?" He wasn't yelling, only his eyes were. "I've got four men outside watching the place. I about have a heart attack every time the phone rings, because I never know how I'm going to get to an extension when you answer it without looking like a total jerk. There's..."

Catching himself he took a deep breath. Saying there was some idiot hiding outside wouldn't help the present situation at all. Curbing his frustration over having to wait for that guy to make a move, he continued with, "On top of that, I've spent half the day trying to be charming to a woman who makes Clarence Darrow look like a first year law student...and the other half trying to avoid setting a date for my 'wedding.'"

She almost felt sorry for him. Almost. "You got the easy part. At least you had the advantage of knowing something about me." His memory had astounded her. Somehow he'd managed to remember everything she'd told the officer at the station—the schools she'd attended, places she'd visited or lived, people she knew. "How do you think I felt when Mom started asking me about your aunt in Maryland? I didn't even know you *had* an aunt in Maryland!"

One second she'd been leaning against the desk. The next, she was being turned around by the shoulders and pushed into the chair Creed had just vacated. "What are you doing?"

"Just sit there and listen," he ordered, and handed her the glass she'd set on the desk. "Just to keep things from getting more awkward than they already are, I'll give you a crash course on Creed Diogenes McAllister."

"Diogenes?"

"My mother's Greek. Your mother already knows that."

"Oh."

"Your mother already knows more about me than I thought *I* knew, but there's a couple things she hasn't gotten to yet." Muttering, "Though God only knows what," he started to pace. "Somehow we'll clear this whole thing up later, but in the meantime..."

The delicate rap on the double doors just before one of them swung open announced the end of their conversation. Britt felt strangely disappointed. Despite the indifferent look she'd managed, she'd actually been looking forward to his "crash course."

"I hope I'm not interrupting anything." Helen glanced from Creed who'd jerked his head toward her, to Britt, who was peering around the wing of the chair.

"Of course not, Mom. Couldn't you rest?"

"I tried." A warm smile crinkled her eyes, erasing her usual air of cool refinement. "I just had too many things on my mind."

Like my wedding, Britt moaned to herself, though she managed a commendably calm smile of her own.

Creed, slipping into his role with all the ease of a seasoned actor, raised his glass. "We were just having a drink before dinner. Care to join us?"

"I'd love to. I'll get my jacket and be right back. It's a bit chilly down here."

The second her mother left, Britt was out of the chair and at Creed's side. Barely noticing the slight lift of his eyebrow, she curled her fingers over his forearm. "What am I going to do?" she whispered, not caring if he heard the note of desperation in her tone.

His response was clipped. "You're going to try to think of some way to get her out of here."

"She's not going to leave until we set a date!"

"She can't stay here forever."

"You don't know my mother."

"Then give her a date."

"I can't do that!"

"Why not?"

"Because it's dishonest! This whole situation is one big lie and I can't hurt my mother like this!"

The muscle in his jaw jerked. Pulling her grip from his arm, he grasped her fingers in his fist. She didn't like the look in his eyes, or the way her body was reacting to the leashed power she could feel in his. He had her pressed back against the desk and the heat of his thighs burned through the thin cotton of her skirt.

"You tell me what other choice we've got, then. Do you want to tell her the truth? Go ahead if you think it'll make you feel better. But you'd also better keep in mind how she's going to feel about being dragged in on all of this, because if you tell her, I won't let her leave here until this is all over. After you've thought about that," he continued in that same tight whisper, "think about telling her that, the way things stand right now, the next time she sees you there's a good possibility it'll be either in a courtroom or from the other side of a row of bars. How do you think she'll feel then? Proud?"

A fair amount of Britt's color had vanished beneath the open collar of her blouse. Stunned by his fierce expression and very aware of his painful grip, all she could manage was a strangled, "You're hurting me."

The blue of his eyes was nearly black when he glanced at the slender fingers clutched in his large hand. Slowly he eased the pressure.

That was his only concession.

"Your mother will be back down here any minute," he hissed. "You've got just that long to decide what you're going to do. I can play it either way."

He could play it either way. She couldn't help but wonder if he realized how appropriate his words were. For the past several hours, she'd felt like an actress who'd stepped onto a stage where all the players knew their lines—except her. Everything that had happened the past few days had seemed a little unreal. Now, that unreality took on more frightening proportions. She felt as if she'd just entered the twilight zone.

Some alien voice used her mouth to form a faint, "Why are you doing this?"

"Because I want to help you."

She was sure of it now. She'd stepped into some weird "otherworld." A second ago he'd looked as if he wanted to strangle her. If his grip had been on her neck instead of her hand, he probably would have succeeded. Now his head had inched lower and it looked very much as if he was going to kiss her.

Because of that odd, otherworldly feeling, she didn't bother to move. "Why?" she whispered.

The words he muttered a scant inch above her mouth brought her back to a nearer dimension. "I'll be damned if I know. But that's not the point now, anyway." The sound of her mother's footsteps crossing the entry added a new note of urgency to his quiet demand. "What are you going to do, Britt?"

Chapter Seven

Helen sat in the breakfast nook, oblivious to the breeze ruffling the orange curtains behind her and the robins singing in the cherry tree outside the window. Her briskly efficient air was compounded by the gold-rimmed half-glasses perched on her nose.

Tapping her pen against the table, she scanned the sheets of lined yellow paper lying in front of her. The frown pleating her forehead was hardly one of displeasure. She was in her element and, to Britt's dismay, was clearly having a ball.

Her mother loved to organize. The reputation she'd earned as a hostess was the envy of Boston society, not to mention any person who'd ever chaired a committee. Those who weren't blessed with Helen Chandler's talents constantly sought her—everyone from the president of the local symphony to the director of the Orphans' Relief Fund. Helen didn't mind at all. Just mention that a function was being planned and she was immediately at the helm.

Like now. Ever since she'd gotten up that morning, she'd been compiling page after page of heaven-only-knew-what. As the number of pages grew, so did Britt's feelings of guilt.

"Don't you want to take a break for lunch, Mom?"

The gray-streaked auburn head remained lowered over the table. "Mmmm...I don't think so. You two go ahead."

Attempts at diversion were useless. Britt knew nothing short of the Second Coming would pry her mother away from her task. Once she got started on her lists, there was no stopping her.

Replacing the lid on the mayonnaise, Britt sent a pleading look in Creed's direction. He was sitting at the counter, his chin propped in his hand while he watched her mix a tuna salad. All he did was smile, and shrug.

Some accomplice he'd turned out to be. They were supposed to be in this together, but he wasn't any help at all. She'd tried to tell him that just setting a date wouldn't be enough; that her mother wouldn't leave until every detail had been worked out, but of course, he hadn't listened.

Slapping a leaf of lettuce down on a white china plate, she tried to tell herself how angry she was. It lacked any degree of conviction, though, she wasn't angry at all. She couldn't even summon up a little self-righteous indignation. Creed was acting as if there actually was going to be a wedding. To her consternation, she was finding it surprisingly easy to act that way herself.

Years of undercover work had obviously given him this talent for deception. But what was her excuse?

"When do you think you'll be able to reach your parents, Creed?" Helen pushed a completed list aside and finally glanced up. "Either of these dates is fine, but until I know which one's convenient for them, I can't order the invitations, or reserve the church, or do much of anything else for that matter."

Thank God for small favors, Britt sighed to herself and shoved an uncut sandwich, on whole wheat, toward Creed. There was no sense letting him know she wasn't completely opposed to what was going on. She liked being able to touch him whenever she felt like it—just as any "engaged" woman would. It was strange how she found herself craving the small caresses he was so free with. At least he was free with them whenever her mother was around. The few times her mother hadn't been present, he hadn't come anywhere near her.

She slid onto the stool beside him, gratified with the way he scowled down at his plate. He hated wheat bread.

"Like I said," he evaded, "they're out on a boat right now and it's a little difficult to reach them."

The boat he was referring to was actually a yacht belonging to some obscure European royalty. His parents were invited guests. Britt's mother had loved that.

"Well, I suppose there's not much we can do about it at the moment." Another list was drawn toward her. "We'll have DeVico's do the catering for the reception. They have an excellent pastry chef. There'll be groom's cake, of course, and since chocolate is your favorite, Creed, we can have the wedding cake made of a couple of layers of that. The other layers should be white though, with lemon filling."

Creed mumbled, "Sounds fine," just before he took a bite of his sandwich.

"Isn't the bride supposed to decide that sort of thing?" Britt inquired. She really didn't care what kind of cake it was, since there wasn't going to be one. If she sat silent, though, her mother might get suspicious. It wasn't her nature to just sit back and let decisions be made for her. Especially over something as important as her "wedding."

Helen obviously appreciated her daughter's conservative side. "You certainly have the final word on this, and all white is more traditional. I just thought it would be nice to get the groom's opinion."

The "groom" glanced down at his plate. "Especially when the bride would want carrot cake made with whole wheat flour."

"I would not..." Britt started to protest, but found her words dissolving the same way her defenses had every time he'd touched her today. His finger pressed against her lips and she was vaguely aware of her mother's satisfied smile.

The tender light in Creed's eyes wasn't for the benefit of Britt's mother. Helen couldn't see it. "You would, too," he teased, moving his finger over Britt's lower lip. "You'd do something like that just to be different."

Her eyes fell to the skirt of her gauzy white shirtwaist. She started toying with the black button on the pocket. There was no reason for her heart to be carrying on the way it was. This was all just a big charade, so why get all bothered over the way his slightest touch affected her? Her feelings had to be just as imaginary as this farce of an engagement. Didn't they?

"Chocolate's fine," she muttered, and added under her breath, "just have them bake a file in it."

Helen didn't hear her, but the way the corners of Creed's mouth were twitching told her he had.

The papers on the table rustled, drawing Britt's attention from the lump of tuna salad she'd been rearranging on her plate. "I can't do much more until Creed talks to his parents," Helen pronounced, gathering her lists. "There is something you and I can do this afternoon, though."

Britt couldn't imagine what that "something" could be. As far as she was concerned everything was on hold for the time being. Relatively comfortable with the knowledge that, so far, this wedding was nothing more than a bunch of things written down on paper, she returned, "What's that?"

"Your gown. We're going shopping."

Creed stiffened. Britt felt rather than saw it. Though it was barely noticeable, she caught the sharp, negative shake of his head.

She couldn't go anywhere. She knew that as well as he did.

Creed had handled this same problem last night when her mother, in her usual inimitable style, had suggested they all go out to dinner. It hadn't been a suggestion at all; she'd been insisting that she take them out.

Creed had neatly circumvented that insistence by appealing to Helen's sense of maternal duty. After all, what mother would want to eat in a restaurant when her daughter had a gourmet meal planned in her honor?

Britt could have shot him. All the time she'd been scraping together that "gourmet meal"—which turned out to be nothing more than a shrimp quiche and spinach salad—she'd seriously considered it. The white roses and baby's breath her mother had suggested for a wedding bouquet could easily be worked into a funeral wreath. Britt would have told Creed so if he'd said one word about the meatless meal. Wisely, he'd kept his mouth shut.

Now, it was Britt's turn to come up with a plausible reason for not leaving the house. At least she didn't have to resort to a lie. "I'm really not in the mood to try on gowns, Mom."

Helen smoothed the collar of her peacock-blue silk blouse. "That's nonsense. There's no such thing as a woman who isn't in the mood to look for her wedding gown. We need to shop for bridesmaids' dresses, too." Her brow creased. "I suppose you'll want Samantha for your maid of honor. I just hope she's not showing much by then."

Samantha Worthington-Lodge—Sammi to those who'd known her before she'd settled down and married Herbert Wallace Lodge—was Britt's dearest friend. She was also the most prolific of her married acquaintances. At twenty-five, and three years married, Samantha was working on her third child. Britt thought it was wonderful.

"I don't really care if she's the size of a house," she countered, momentarily forgetting that it didn't make any difference anyway. "I'm still not in the mood to shop today."

"Fine." Helen crossed the kitchen and poured her cold coffee in the sink. Britt frowned at her back. Her mother never gave in that easily, and immediately proved it. "We'll go tomorrow then."

Since Helen was facing the other direction, Creed didn't need to guard his warning glance. There was nothing remotely subtle about the message Britt received from those narrowed blue eyes. He was clearly telling her, *Do something!*

The brown eyes that held his for that challenging instant spoke a message equally clear. She'd tried to tell him it wasn't going to be easy getting her mother out of here. Maybe now he'd believe her.

Using the only argument she could think of that might make her mother back off a bit, she leaned forward and crossed her arms on the counter. "Don't you think we'd do better looking for dresses back in Boston? It would make it easier for the . . . ah, the rest of the party."

"I'd thought of that, but it would be fun to look here, too."

There was so much anticipation in Helen's eyes that Britt felt positively awful. She hated to dampen that excitement, but this whole thing was growing ridiculously out of proportion. "It would be fun," she conceded graciously, "but I really think we should wait until I get back home. Besides, you were supposed to meet Dad this morning and, since you've done everything you can here, I think we should call the airline and see about getting you on a plane. It's not every day you go to Hawaii, you know."

Helen looked petulant, an odd expression to see on someone who'd seen the better part of fifty years. "I was in Hawaii three months ago." Absently, she inspected a miniscule chip in her nail polish. "It really wouldn't hurt to start looking for your gown here, you know."

Some very expensive orthodontic work was put to the stress test when Britt gritted her teeth. Creed's hand folded over her thigh. The gentle squeeze of his fingers seemed to say, *Hang in there.* His slight nod said, *You're doing fine.*

She wasn't doing fine at all. Whether he knew it or not, the way his fingers were now wandering up and down the length of her skirt, gently massaging the firm flesh beneath it, was making it a little difficult to think. What he was doing wasn't necessary. The counter hid his actions from Helen.

Picking up his hand, Britt placed it firmly back in his lap and launched into a discourse of the advantages of shopping in Boston.

The ensuing mother-daughter debate, as friendly as it was, would have bored Creed to distraction if he hadn't been so interested in the outcome. Neither Britt nor her mother seemed to have any clear advantage—not surprising considering that they were equally opinionated. He could see now why Britt had that irritating, and rather endearing, rebellious streak. Beneath Helen Chandler's feminine, manicured exterior lay the heart of a very domineering woman. It was a dominance tempered with love, but he could see how stifling that kind of love could be. Britt hadn't had any choice but to assert her independence.

Knowing how highly she valued that independence, he couldn't help but admire her for the way she'd been handling herself. She was in a situation where she had no control, yet she was in complete control of herself.

"...it would just be a waste of time for me to go to Hawaii now," Helen concluded.

Britt, acutely conscious of Creed's eyes on her, kept hers fixed on her mother's determined expression. "Not necessarily. You could do me a favor while you're over there." Helen's eyebrows rose expectantly. "I want my gown to be something special. Unique. Maybe you could shop around for a gown on Maui. If you find something you think I'd like, have the shop send me a picture. If it's right, you can pick it up."

She'd just played her last hand. There was nothing else she could think of that would placate her mother about this wedding gown business *and* get her on that plane.

Britt never had been much of a card player. But even a novice knew when she'd drawn a handful of aces—and one joker.

Readily agreeing with the suggestion, and announcing that Britt had just given her a wonderful idea, Helen started preparing another set of lists. Since the earliest flight she could get didn't leave until nine that evening, there was plenty of time to draw up an alternate set of plans. Something really unusual for Boston: a formal wedding with a tropical theme. Helen loved themes.

At least Creed had the decency to muffle his groan when he slid off the stool and disappeared through the louvered doors.

Tablet in hand, her mother headed in the opposite direction. "I'm going to get some sun while I work on this," she explained, attributing her daughter's pained expression to bridal nerves. Seconds later, she'd vanished outside to settle herself on a chaise by the pool.

Britt decided it wasn't worth the effort to point out how little sun her mother would get wearing a long sleeved blouse and slacks. She was just grateful to find herself alone with her misery.

Concentrating on the mechanics of clearing away the lunch dishes, she tried to simply blank her mind. The attempt, valiant as it was, failed resoundingly. Oddly enough, it wasn't the dread she was feeling about eventually having to tell her mother that the "wedding" was off that was making her so miserable. Nor was it the constant fear that her mother might be in the room the next time the phone rang, and it would be Mr. Barnes calling. It wasn't even the nagging sense of helplessness she felt over not being able to prove her innocence and convince Creed's men they were wrong about her. It was Creed.

She kept reminding herself that he was only doing his job, and part of that job called upon his extraordinarily convincing acting abilities. With his coaching, she'd been putting on a pretty good show herself.

Britt hadn't been acting though. Somewhere along the line the feelings she was trying to pretend for her mother's benefit had started to become very real.

"Gratitude," she muttered, squishing a piece of cellophane wrap over the tuna salad she hadn't eaten. It was perfectly logical to feel grateful to him. After all, he was protecting her by keeping the truth from her mother. He was also keeping her out of jail—for the time being. Telling herself that was all she felt toward Creed, she shoved the plate into the refrigerator.

Her attempts at rationalization weren't working. Gratitude didn't make a person's knees want to buckle when someone smiled at them. It didn't make a person's blood turn to steam when that someone touched them, either. Rather than getting into an argument with herself over that inescapable logic, she leaned over the sink to look at the window and tried to focus her attention on the woman thoughtfully creating her lists. Helen was so preoccupied that she didn't even notice that the sun she'd gone outside to get was rapidly vanishing behind some very ominous-looking clouds.

"She's really gotten into this, hasn't she?"

Out of sheer necessity, Britt had been practicing the ability Creed had to quickly camouflage his feelings. That practice paid off. Since several seconds had intervened between her last thoughts of him and her present ones, all he saw when she turned was frustration—and daughterly guilt. "I tried to tell you what would happen, but you wouldn't listen."

Jamming his hands into his pockets, he stepped beside her to peer out the window. "Count your blessings, honey. She was willing to settle for a couple of months or so. My mom would have had us married yesterday."

That thought was far too appealing. "I guess it's a good thing it wasn't your mother who showed up then."

The defense in her tone was directed at herself, but he didn't know that. She met his own frustration when she moved away and he dropped the edge of the orange curtain he'd been holding back. "Don't, Britt."

"Don't what?"

The Clydesdales galloping through the beer logo on his T-shirt seemed to grow larger with his indrawn breath. "You've made it plain enough how you feel about all this. If you have to expound on that opinion, I'd appreciate it if you'd wait until after she leaves."

"I wasn't going to expound on anything."

The horse-drawn wagon centered on the logo was obliterated by the muscular forearms folding over it. "Come on, Britt," he drawled. "I know you better than that."

"Do you?" she challenged, and saw him frown when she didn't give him the argument he was so sure she wanted.

Rather than risk tackling that question, he chose to amend the subject. "I'm definitely beginning to know your mother, anyway. Has she always been so thorough?"

Nodding gravely, she raised her hand to push back the curls that had fallen over her cheek.

Creed's hand beat hers. Moving her fingers away, he tucked the soft curls behind her ear. "You know—" a waving tendril was curled around his thumb "—the only thing she hasn't done is ask what size I wear. I keep expecting her to ask for a tape measure so she can order my tuxedo."

Britt swallowed when his hand snaked toward her nape. Her throat felt a bit tight. "Give her time. She'll think of it sooner or later."

The motion outside the window caught his attention. "Oh, God," he groaned. "It looks like she's just thought of something."

Indeed it did. Helen's strides were carrying her purposefully toward the house.

"Come here." One swift jerk and Britt found herself smashed up against the Clydesdales. The feel of his hand pressing into the small of her back and his hard chest crushed to hers sent her heart on a rampaging gallop. "Maybe her sense of propriety will make her go away."

There had scarcely been enough time to react, let alone think. Propriety? The word rattled dumbly in her mind as his mouth anchored over hers.

Wanting to bury the responses aching to be felt, she told herself this was just part of his act—and something she shouldn't be enjoying, either. But when she heard the backdoor open, then close, and her mother's retreating footsteps on the concrete outside, she found herself giving in to her... gratitude.

She'd expected him to pull away when her mouth softened. Instead, his own became more pliant. Insistent. His purpose had been served, but the demands issuing from his tongue when it plunged into the welcoming sweetness she offered spoke of another purpose.

He hadn't kissed her like this since the day at the falls. Was that only two days ago? some vaguely coherent part of her asked. Reason faltered, then vanished. It had been an eternity.

Angling her body to his advantage, he thrust his thighs boldly against her. Britt sought every contact he offered, and more. She relished his masculine scent, the surprisingly soft texture of his hair, the smooth-rough feel of his face. She wanted to know every detail of the lines feathering from the corners of his eyes, the deeper ones bracketing the mouth that seemed so reluctant to leave hers when he dropped tender kisses to her eyes, her jaw, and the lobe of her ear.

His fingers teased, then lifted the weight of her breast. "Oh, honey," he breathed, the heat of his tongue tracing her ear sending an erratic pattern of shivers down her neck. "It's a damn good thing we're not alone."

She wasn't going to play coy and ask him why. She knew. What she didn't know was why she wasn't agreeing with him. "We'll be alone tonight," she murmured against the base of his throat. The pulse there jerked beneath her lips.

Catching the hair at her nape, he drew her head back, his eyes blazing with the same fire that burned in her. The question in those searing depths didn't need to be verbalized.

Neither did her equally silent response. Her eyes, dark with invitation and desire, caressed the tense contours of his face, touched the sensual line of his mouth, and settled steadily on his.

A tight groan rumbled deep in his chest, the faint vibration echoing the length of her body. The kiss she wanted so badly was buried in her hair and he just held her, soothed her, until Helen's unnecessarily loud cough outside the door warned them of her intended return.

"Sixteen collar and thirty-four sleeve," Creed replied to Helen's hurried request for his shirt size. He pointedly ignored Britt's droll smile.

Helen readjusted her tablet against the edge of the banister. Her luggage was already in the cab; the cabbie probably grinning at the running meter. All afternoon Helen had been insisting she was forgetting something, and had looked enormously pleased when she'd finally remembered it just when the cab arrived to take her to the airport.

A wing of carefully penciled auburn eyebrow arched. "Slacks?"

"Thirty-four square," came the indulgent reply from below her.

Creed was sitting on the bottom step. Britt was leaning against the gilded side table by the front door.

"Well, that should ... No wait. What about shoes?"

Creed overlooked a more flippant response and dutifully replied, "Eleven-D."

"Hat size?"

"What do you need that for?"

This time it was her mother who looked indulgent. "Your top hat."

"I don't want one."

"Oh, Creed, of course you do. You can't wear tails without a ..."

"Seven," he cut in, recalling the information from his days in uniform. The last thing he wanted to do was delay her departure by getting into a debate over a top hat of all things.

"Good." Helen stuffed the tablet into her briefcase-size leather purse. "Now, as soon as you've decided on your groomsmen, you'll call me with their measurements, all right?" It was hardly a request. More of a polite order. "This will all come in handy in case you can't get the right tuxedos here. I really wish you could find a tape measure, Brittany. It would be so much more accurate if I could . . ."

"You're going to miss your plane, Mom." Britt's affectionate smile took the rudeness from her interruption.

At the reminder, Helen's glance flew to her watch and she to the door. "I didn't realize it was getting so late. Your father will have a fit if I miss my flight." A quick kiss was placed on Britt's cheek and she was enveloped in a rose-scented hug. "I'll call you from Maui, dear."

Another round of hugs, this one including Creed, a warning for the two of them to behave themselves, which sounded quite serious, and the cab finally pulled out from under the portico. Her mother could still be seen waving from the back window when the taxi disappeared around the hedges lining the drive.

"I know this isn't going to sound right," Creed sighed, closing the door when Britt stepped back inside, "but I don't think I've ever been so happy to see anyone leave."

A rueful smile lit her eyes. "You don't have to apologize. I know exactly what you mean." Bending down, she picked up a leaf the moisture-heavy breeze had blown in. From the feel of the air outside, they were in for a storm. The clouds she'd noticed earlier had been growing heavier all day. "Under any other circumstances, I think you might have liked her."

"I don't *dis*like her," he quickly corrected, watching Britt trace the veins in the curled oak leaf with her finger. "It's just like you said. The circumstances weren't exactly ideal. I guess the part that really got to me is that I'm not used to . . ." He cut himself off, and frowned.

Since it looked as if he was mulling over a variety of potential complaints, she simplified his choices by offering, "Having your life organized for you?"

"Yeah," he nodded, thoughtfully. Pushing himself away from where he'd been leaning against the door, he took the step that placed him in front of her. "Is that what you had to contend with all the time you were growing up?"

When she shook her head, three curls sprang defiantly from the black ribbon that was supposed to be holding them back. Knowing they'd just reassert themselves again, she didn't bother to push them away. "She's mellowed a lot in the past few years."

"She used to be worse?"

Britt couldn't help but smile at his slightly appalled expression. "Much. Don't get the wrong idea, though. Everything she does, she does because she cares. It's because of her concern that she wants everything to be perfect."

One thick black eyebrow arched expressively. "Even her daughter?"

Britt laughed. "I was one of her less-than-perfect projects, I'm afraid." Looking up from the leaf she'd been unconsciously shredding, her pulse picked up that all-too-familiar beat. He was staring at her mouth.

"Maybe I have a different opinion."

The quiet delivery of his statement put an immediate and effective end to the conversation about the woman who was no longer there—the woman whose presence had curbed the subtle sexual tension that had been increasing for the better part of the day. Though that tension had always been there, until now it hadn't seemed quite so perceptible, so acute. There was nothing to alleviate the electricity leaping between them now.

It was almost a tangible thing. Heavy. Enervating. Senses sprang to life, identifying every sensation, every sound filling the silence surrounding them.

Their eyes locked, and held.

Through the dull pounding in her ears, Britt was vaguely aware of the rhythmic tick of the grandfather clock behind her, the surge of wind pelting the first drops of rain against the house. She became aware of her breath, rapid and shallow, and her breasts, which seemed to swell when his eyes lowered to linger upon them.

Her skin grew warm as his eyes and his tongue, touching his lips, suggested what he'd like to do to those hardening tips. It grew warmer still when that unmasked look traced a slow path over the airy white fabric covering her stomach, her hips, then back up along her bare arms to tenderly caress every inch of her face, her hair.

Trembling from the intimacy of his visual caresses, her gaze faltered, and fell. She saw his forefinger brush his thumb, recalling the way he liked to feel the texture of her curls between them. An odd ache centered in her stomach.

He was making love to her. Though he hadn't physically touched her he was caressing her in a place that was as real and as vital as the slender body containing it. Her soul.

"Creed." She didn't know what else to say—or even what she was trying to express. His whispered name hung suspended until the howl of the gathering wind outside overtook it.

A tiny smile, strangely soft and bittersweet, met the thrilling intensity in his eyes. Drawing a deep breath, he touched her cheek. "I know, honey." His arms encircled her, coaxing her head to lay against his chest. The faintest breath of a kiss was brushed against her temple. "I know."

Did he? Did he know how her heart and her mind were at war with each other? Logic insisted it was only her dependence on him—a dependence necessitated by circumstances far beyond her control—that was blowing her emotions all out of proportion. Her heart and body kept refuting that logic. And her body, melting against the solid strength of his, was issuing a set of demands impossible to ignore.

But Creed was demanding nothing of her. He was just holding her as tightly as she was him, and wishing he hadn't seen the uncertainty shadowing her lovely brown eyes. It would be so easy to give in to the hunger and the urgent physical ache that threatened to obliterate reason.

He shifted, bringing her softness into intimate alignment with his hips. A faint, kittenish moan answered the provocative movement.

It would also be easy to overcome her uncertainty. He knew all the tender little phrases, all the ways to touch a woman to break down the last of her resistance. Britt wasn't fighting him, any resistance she exerted was only against herself. Because of that, he wasn't going to take advantage of the willingness being transmitted by her tentative, tormenting touch. No matter how much he wanted her.

There was something else he had to remember. In their present situation, making love with her would be far too compromising—for both of them. No matter how often he kept forgetting it, she was still a suspect. A beautiful, warm and compelling suspect who was making a mockery of his once-cherished objectivity.

Tipping her chin, he smiled down at her. "How are you at strategy games?"

She blinked, uncomprehending, and eased her hand along his side. "What kind of strategy games?"

He pulled one of the curls away from her ear, brushing the end of it along her jaw. "The kind of games where you try to guess the other person's next move."

If it hadn't been for the contradicting lightness in his husky voice, she might have easily guessed what he would do next. Creed's lips were mere inches from hers. Hoping her voice didn't sound as breathless as she felt, she admitted, "I don't think I'm very good at them."

"Too bad." The corner of her mouth was teased with the feathery end of the curl. "Without any competition, I'll have an easy win."

She stiffened. Her arms fell to her side. Humiliation tore her eyes from the puzzling warmth in his. An easy win? Is that what he thought of her? "Let me go," she whispered harshly.

He tightened his hold. "Easy, honey. I'm talking about chess."

Disbelief vied with hurt, and then the realization that she'd so obviously misunderstood him. "Chess?" Her shoulders went limp beneath his gentle kneading.

"Uh-huh," he nodded with a self-deprecating smile. "You told me the other night you had no intention of letting me be the first man to undress you." Pushing her back, his devilish gaze did just that as it slowly raked her body. "So, unless you've had a change of heart, I think we'd better occupy ourselves with something more, uh . . . intellectual."

Her heart was definitely undergoing some changes. Rapid and drastic ones. But the teasing in his eyes, and the way he was all but shoving her toward the living room, made her keep her admissions to herself—along with the relief she felt at not having to deal with them right now. All she would admit when he put the chessboard on the coffee table and indicated the spot on the floor where she should sit, was, "I haven't played chess since I was a kid."

"Looks like I've got a few things to teach you then."

The gleam in his eyes was far too wicked to mean anything about the game they were about to play. Knowing she needed to do something to alleviate the subtle tension still darting between them, she reached for one of the pieces on the board. Her hand settled on a white knight, her expression growing thoughtful as she fingered the delicately carved ivory.

Creed had settled opposite her, and a knowing smile creased his darkly attractive features. "Don't draw mental analogies, Britt." Taking the white knight from her, he turned the board around, giving her the black pieces. "We both know what would be happening right now if our circumstances were any different than they are. Just for the record . . . my thoughts are far from honorable."

The air fairly crackled with the same electricity nature displayed beyond the curtained windows, adding an exciting intimacy to the sense of companionship that eventually settled between them. Until the lights went out.

Chapter Eight___

There had been no warning flicker from the lamps. Just a flash of lightning, the rumble of thunder competing with the scream of the wind, then total darkness.

Creed's muttered profanity was followed by the sound of something hard—his knee—hitting the underside of the coffee table. Another oath joined the first.

"You don't have to get so upset just because it was your move," Britt teased, reaching behind her for the edge of the sofa. "Ouch!"

"What was that?"

"My shin."

"Sorry. What're you doing?"

"I'm trying to get up, but your foot's on my skirt."

"Where do you think you're going?"

She gave her skirt a jerk. The motion was unnecessary; Creed had already moved his foot. "To get a candle." A second later she heard something thump against the carpet. It sounded heavy—like the crystal ashtray that had been sitting on the edge of the coffee table. "Stay put before you break something," she sighed and pulled herself to her feet.

Creed said nothing, though she could hear him moving again.

Groping along the sofa, she felt for the end table and tried to remember how far it was to the fireplace. Four steps? Five? Her fingers jammed against the bricks. Three steps. It was her turn to mutter this time. She'd just broken a nail.

A tense chuckle came from somewhere behind her. "Be careful."

She grumbled a dry, "Thanks," and slowly worked her fingers along the mantel. She found what she was looking for. There were only a couple inches of taper left in the brass candlestick, but it was enough. "Got it," she pronounced, triumphant. "Where are you?"

"Right here."

"Cute, Creed. Where's right here?"

"How the hell am I supposed to know? It's dark in here."

"You're kidding." Her droll reply held the hint of a smile. "We need matches. There's some down here somewhere."

"Where?"

"By the fireplace tools. They're in a brass . . ."

"Got 'em. Hold out your hand."

"I am holding it out. The candle's in it. Creed!"

"What?"

"That's not the candle."

"Really?" His hand drifted from where it was shaping her calf, his voice coming from above her now. "I thought all candles felt like that."

"Are you going to light this thing?" Actually, she thought, a match probably wouldn't be necessary. The warm feel of his fingers on her bare skin had been a potent reminder of the fire she'd been busily suppressing for the better part of two hours. If she held the candle much longer, it would either melt or light itself.

The flare of a long match illuminated his smiling yet oddly strained features. "Get the other one," he instructed, taking the candle she held and nodding toward the one sitting farther down the mantel. "Let's see if the phone's out, too."

A white streak of lightning creased the sky, coinciding with a great crack of thunder. "Sound's like it's right over us." Creed spoke the observation absently and touched her wick to his. It sputtered, then flared. "Come on."

Shivering a little as the beat of the rain grew louder, she followed him into the study. Britt loved storms. There was an intense, primitive force about them that she found as fascinating as the man whose features were shadowed from her.

"Just stay in your cars until it passes," Creed was saying into the phone. "Is Alexander still there?" Alexander was the code name they'd given to the man who seemed to come and go from the woods with all the ease of a phantom. The officer on the other end of the line told Creed what he already knew. At the moment, there was no way to know for sure. Unless the guy was a fool though, he had probably gone someplace a little drier.

Creed never had trusted the obvious.

Replacing the receiver, he sucked in a frustrated breath and glanced at Britt. She was leaning against the desk, her profile barely visible through the cloud of auburn hair burnished by the flickering candlelight. Bathed in that soft golden glow, she had an ethereal, almost haunting quality about her. Elusive, and terribly sensual. Though he couldn't see them, he knew the intelligence in her eyes and could almost hear the wheels turning inside her head. He couldn't help but wonder what thoughts were contained behind those long and lowered lashes. A question was forming there, he was certain of that.

"Who's Alexander?"

Refraining from silently congratulating himself for being able to read her so well, he edged around the desk. "One of the men outside." He was comfortable with the evasion, but not with the thought of what he had to do now.

"I don't suppose they're too happy about this." The wide arc of her hand indicated the storm raging outside. "Just because they don't believe me doesn't mean they deserve to come down with pneumonia. Do you want to ask them to come in until the rain stops?"

At her thoughtfulness, he smiled inwardly, but his tone was flat. "They're fine."

"Boy, I'd sure hate to work for you."

"They're used to it."

A troubled frown touched her face. She'd meant her remark to be teasing, like those they'd tossed back and forth all during their rather unorthodox game of chess. Most of the time, Creed had made her moves for her, and she his. She hadn't thought of it at the time, but the way they'd played left no way for either side to win. She didn't want to think about that now. She was too concerned with how serious Creed had become. The more she thought about that, the more she realized how much his mood had changed in the past few minutes—ever since the lights had gone out.

The quiet companionship they'd shared suddenly seemed strained. By mutual, unspoken agreement, they hadn't talked of the investigation or the little scenario they'd played out for her mother. For a couple of hours they'd just been two people enjoying each other's company. Now they were once again immersed in the reality that had thrown them together in the first place.

Her candle danced wildly as she pushed herself away from the desk. "It's getting late."

"You going to bed?"

She nodded, watching his shadow follow him when he stepped toward her.

"I'll come up, too."

His words were clipped, but because his back was to her while he reached for the candle he'd left sitting on the desk, she couldn't see the shuttered coolness in his eyes. She didn't have to. She knew it was there.

The honeymoon was over.

Creed followed her through the house while she locked up, a task made more tedious by the lack of light. His wick had burned down and Britt's was threatening to by the time they reached the top of the stairs.

"I'll get ready for bed, then you can have this one," Britt offered, referring to the remaining candle. "I'll hurry."

Creed had said little during the past few minutes, and all she got now was a nod from the shadows before he stepped into the darkness of his room.

Squelching a curse when his leg hit the footboard of his bed, Creed sank to the edge of the mattress. His night vision was excellent, but he'd just been too preoccupied to pay attention to what he was doing. He wasn't really concentrating now, either, as shirt, shoes and socks were tossed toward the outline of an overstuffed chair. The shoes hit the floor with a thud. He couldn't tell where the shirt and socks landed.

The way he saw it, he had two choices. He could either insist that she keep her door open and he could stay awake all night listening for the sounds of something that might not even happen, or he could sleep in her room. At least that way he could get some rest and if something did happen, he'd be there.

He almost laughed out loud at his rationale. Did he honestly think he'd be able to get any rest with her sleeping only feet, or inches, away?

There was one other little problem with that choice. When he'd baited her about sharing her room before, she'd made it quite clear where he'd sleep. He, however, had no intention of sleeping in the bathtub—or on the floor for that matter. He was tired, and tense, and suddenly in no mood for any kind of an argument.

He was getting angry. With the Barneses for dragging Britt into this. With Britt for not having the sense to see what she was getting herself into when she took this house-sitting job. With "Alexander" for the unknown threat he represented. And with the electric company for taking so long to fix the damn power lines.

More than anything else though, he was angry with himself—for being angry. He'd always kept a lid on his emotions. In his line of work, it was not only advisable, but necessary. Unfortunately, it was not always possible.

Stuffing his pillow under his arm, he avoided the footboard and stepped out into the hall. The best night vision in the world wouldn't have helped him here. It was pitch black.

"Britt?"

He heard her door opening a foot away and stepped toward the sound.

The sliver of candle, its flame lagging, was thrust toward him. The faint yellow light made his scowl look almost sinister, his eyes silver and harsh. "I hurried," she said defensively, chalking up the chill running down her spine to nothing more than the startling boom of thunder.

At first she thought it was only the unreliable light that made him look so fierce. But when he pushed past her, she could almost feel the tension radiating from him. He didn't seem irritated. It was more like plain old mad.

Which made Britt wary. Just because she was becoming quite familiar with his moods didn't mean she trusted them. "What's the matter?"

When he didn't answer and tossed his pillow down on her bed, she tried again, more skeptical than ever. "What are you doing?"

He'd stretched out on the bed, his jean covered legs crossed at the ankle and his bronzed torso appearing even darker next to the white sheets. "I'm going to get some sleep," he mumbled, throwing his forearm over his eyes.

Strangely reluctant to utter the protest she knew he was expecting, she stared down at his long frame. It had taken her only minutes to change into the short ivory nylon nightshirt she was wearing, but those minutes had brought on an odd, almost eerie feeling. The storm didn't really bother her; neither did the lack of electricity. It was just that in the relatively unfamiliar house, every creak of the structure groaning against the wind had seemed magnified. It was ridiculous to be frightened. And she wasn't, not exactly. Just . . . uneasy.

Creed's presence—even though his attitude left something to be desired—seemed to lessen that uncomfortable feeling.

She knew she should tell him to go, but all she heard herself doing was asking him, "Why?"

"Because I'm tired," came his terse reply.

"I didn't mean that." Her eyes flicked over the soft swirl of black curls tapering down his chest. Just as her gaze reached the beltless waistband of his jeans, her candle sputtered and died. "I meant, why here?"

From out of the darkness, he replied dryly, "Because I'm afraid of the dark."

She didn't believe that for a second. His reason had to be something much less obvious. Creed didn't seem to do anything without a reason, but his purpose now completely escaped her. His sarcasm, his coolness, erased any possibility of a seduction attempt. So what was going on?

Asking him would get her nowhere. Though she couldn't see a thing, she could feel the wall he'd thrown up between them.

In spite of that wall, or maybe because of it, she moved carefully toward the bed. "You're on my side," she informed him, unable to believe how calm she sounded.

Creed couldn't believe it either. Moving over, he felt the mattress give beneath her slight weight. He'd been bracing himself for an argument and felt ridiculously disappointed that she hadn't given him one. Maybe he didn't know her as well as he thought he did.

She mumbled, "Sorry," when her fingers grazed the bare skin of his side and jerked her hand back to shove it under the pillow. Turning her back to him, she heard his soft expulsion of breath.

"Britt?"

"Hmmm?"

For a moment there was nothing but silence. The quiet silence of the rain and the wind and her heart beating in her ears. Then, the sound of a smile mingling with Creed's quietly whispered, "Goodnight."

The stillness in the room woke Britt. The storm had abated, leaving a pale crescent of moon to illuminate the features of the man curled up beside her. Her head was nestled in the curve of his arm, his leg lying heavily over hers. The gentle rhythm of his deep, even breath made his chest rise and fall beneath her hand.

She had no idea what time it was, or when they had reached for each other in their sleep. She only knew how right it felt to be held by him, to touch him. His mouth, slightly parted, looked so vulnerable, but even in repose his brow furrowed as if troubled by his dreams. She touched the skin between his eyebrows, running her fingers lightly upward to soothe those unknown tensions.

Something else felt right, too. But in that misty plane between sleep and consciousness, the word didn't form. Her hand fell limply to his cheek.

The next time she woke, Creed was gone.

Showered and dressed, Britt ventured back to her bedroom window, sipping her tea as she peeked through the curtains. Creed was still doing laps. He'd been at them a lot longer than usual this morning.

Absently placing her cup on the dresser, she watched his lean, muscular form glide effortlessly back and forth across the pool. Every movement was powerful and controlled. "Like the man himself," she said to the empty room, and pressed her forehead to the glass.

She'd never met a man like him. All the others she'd known had been so...so malleable. She was certain there must be some strong types among the artists and intellectuals she'd dated, but if there were, they'd managed to hide it from her. Britt had never wanted a man she could dominate. She didn't want one who would dominate her, either. She'd had enough of that while she was growing up to last a lifetime. What she wanted was an equal, someone she could share with.

She wanted Creed.

When she wasn't fighting him, and he wasn't asserting his professional authority, they seemed to move in perfect sync. There'd been times during the past couple of days when they'd anticipated each other's thoughts or needs with little more than a glance. There had also been times when she could have cheerfully throttled him. He'd evoked every emotion she'd ever thought possible. Anger, frustration, ecstasy... and love.

Her head snapped back from the pane, her fingers clutching the heavy drapery for support as she stared down at Creed. "It can't be," she tried to tell herself. "It just can't."

The denial didn't work, and the shock of realization seemed unduly compounded by the certainty of truth. No wonder it had been so easy to pull off that charade for her mother. She *was* in love with him.

But it didn't make any sense. Love was something that happened over a period of time. Something that grew out of caring and shared experiences. Not something that snuck up on you in less than a week.

Her numb fingers pushed the curtain farther aside. Whether or not what had happened fit her preconceived ideas of its beginning, she couldn't deny the fact. She did love him.

There was another fact that couldn't be denied, either. Creed's only love was his work. He'd told her that much during their drive to the falls. It came before anything else, even before his desire to have a family of his own.

Squeezing her eyes closed, she tried to fight the utter futility of her feelings. Creed's primary interest in her was this case. Anything else was just a physical attraction that would be forgotten as soon as it was closed. His attraction toward her didn't even appear to be that strong. They'd spent the entire night together in her bed and he hadn't even tried . . .

She shook off that thought. She hadn't wanted him to do anything.

There was no comfort to be found in that lie.

When she opened her eyes, Creed was lifting himself to the edge of the pool. His broad shoulders glistened in the morning sun, muscles rippling as he supported his weight easily on his hands and swung himself out. Seconds later, he'd disappeared inside the latticed gazebo.

Britt sank against the sill and let her gaze wander over the leaf-strewn lawn to the heavy stand of trees surrounding the back of the property. Something was moving between the trees. Her eyes fixed on the shape of someone crouched low between two firs. One of Creed's men, she'd dismissed, too preoccupied with her newly discovered feelings to give the dark figure any further thought. If she hadn't been in the middle of an emotional crisis, she might have waved. A minute later, out of sheer perversity, she did.

Creed flipped the towel he'd left on the bench in the gazebo over his shoulder and looked through the lattice-work at Britt's window. She was still there.

Her power to arouse him even from this distance was a little unsettling. It had been even more acute when he'd first awakened to find her curled up in his arms. For a long time he'd just lain there, relishing the feel of the woman circumstance was forbidding him. Minutes later, he'd been counting out laps. There'd been no point in lying there torturing himself.

His eyes narrowed, focusing more clearly on her face. She was staring intently toward the woods, her expression troubled. Then, in a gesture seeming a bit odd since she couldn't possibly see him, she waved.

Following the path her eyes had taken, Creed froze. A few hundred feet away, he saw the dark shape slip into the trees. It wasn't one of his men. He knew exactly where they were.

She'd just waved at Alexander.

Britt heard the back door close and let the curtain fall back over the window. What was she going to do? Part of her felt all the wonder and joy of loving the man she'd waited a lifetime for, yet another part felt only the ache of having to keep that love to herself. Could she do that? Could she face Creed and pretend nothing had changed?

Fairly certain she wouldn't be able to pull off that kind of an act just yet, she dug through her closet for the turquoise sandals that matched the raglan-sleeved blouse she'd tucked into her white slacks. She'd give Creed time to get upstairs to shower and then . . . and then, what?

In the past few minutes her thoughts had scattered like the leaves the wind had torn from the trees last night. Waving at the man outside—she was sure he hadn't liked the idea that she'd seen him—had reminded her of the fishbowl existence she was living. That reminded her of the Barneses and the fact that Mr. Barnes still hadn't called. Then came thoughts of her mother growing hysterical because all her plans were ruined, and then the image of herself stamping out pastel-colored license plates, and Creed calling out that everything would be all right . . . "My God," she groaned, staring blankly at the sandal she hadn't even realized she'd found. "I'm not in love. I'm insane."

That thought drove her to the door. She had to get out of here—away from the confines of the house that felt more and more like a prison. She knew she couldn't go very far, but Creed couldn't possibly object to her taking a walk around the grounds. Not with his men watching every move she made. She wasn't going to ask his permission; he was the last person she wanted to see right now.

One sandal on and the other in her hand, she tore down the stairs.

Creed wasn't in his room, which was where she'd expected him to be. He was in the kitchen, standing in the middle of the puddle he'd dripped on the floor. A thick white towel was draped around his neck and the skimpy blue swim trunks he'd left outside that first morning clung damply to his narrow hips. Britt came to a screeching halt by the counter.

"What's the rush?" His tone was bland, his eyes moving quickly from the paleness of her finely boned face to the sandal she clutched in her hand. He saw the delicate cords of her slender neck convulse as she swallowed. Her eyes seemed to be everywhere but on him.

Those expressive eyes were now on the shoe she was slipping on her foot. "No rush," she replied, trying not to sound agitated.

"That's not the way it looked to me."

The sound escaping her lips might have passed for a laugh had it not been so strained. "Nervous energy, I guess." Straightening, she pushed a handful of curls from her face. It was probably more like a nervous breakdown, but she wasn't going to dwell on that right now.

What she needed to do was get hold of herself and call a little of that masking Boston reserve into play.

The tilt of her head was almost regal when she forced herself to meet his eyes. She held his enigmatic stare for as long as she could—about two and a half seconds— then glanced away.

Creed distractedly reached for the cup of coffee he'd just poured. "Anything interesting going on this morning?"

Other than the fact that I've realized I'm in love with you? she asked silently. "Uh...no," she mumbled. "Aren't you going to get your shower?"

"You trying to get rid of me?" he sounded almost teasing. Almost.

Her eyes darted toward the back door. She wanted desperately to get outside, away from everything. Away from him. If she told him she wanted to go for a walk though, he'd probably want to go with her. "No," she denied quietly. "I was just curious."

Pushing his cup aside, his eyes fixed on hers, searching. For what, she had no idea. "I was just on my way up," he informed her, his expression positively rigid as he moved through the louvered doors.

Seconds later Britt was outside, her chaotic thoughts blinding her to the beauty of the garden, the lushness of the lawns, and the feel of Creed's eyes following her.

The instant she'd gone out, Creed was back in the kitchen on the phone. "Can you see her?"

Through the crackle of the connection patched into the surveillance team's radios, he heard Hollister's crisp, "In sight, Captain. She's headed for the woods."

Creed could see her. She was running now. Straight to the place Alexander had been only a few minutes before.

"Don't do anything until you see them together. It might just be a coincidence."

"Aw, come on, Creed. You aren't still buying that song and dance she's feeding you? I'll bet my badge she's in for a percentage of the take and that guy's just been waiting for her to..."

"You heard me," Creed clipped, cutting off the detective's gravelly voice. A moment later, he broke the connection.

For several seconds he just stood there pressing his fingers to his forehead. He didn't want to accept what he was seeing. But how could he deny what his own eyes told him? Britt had definitely looked anxious, nervous. Maybe she was just getting a bad case of cabin fever. Maybe that was why she...

The excuses his mind was trying to conjure up didn't hold any water. He'd seen her signal Alexander. So had two of his men. And whether he wanted to believe it or not, it did look as if she was on her way to meet him.

Emotions Creed never had to deal with before were fighting an uphill battle with professional instinct. The only feeling he'd acknowledge was the quiet anxiety of having to wait.

It was half an hour before he got the call telling him his men hadn't seen Britt and Alexander together. Britt had been in the woods for only a few minutes, and they hadn't seen Alexander at all. "Maybe she left the money for him," one of the team had suggested.

One of the experts from the search team had given Creed the combination, so he checked the safe before she returned. The marked bills were still there. But so was the feeling that his instincts might have failed him this time. She could have left Alexander a note, a key. She could have been doing just about anything out there....

She'd been chasing a squirrel. A terribly unrefined thing for a grown woman to do, but Britt hadn't cared about refinement or decorum or much of anything else just then. It had felt good to forget about everything for a while and do something simply because she wanted to.

Right now what she wanted to do was work. Ever since she'd returned and swept past Creed's brooding form in the kitchen a couple of hours ago, that's exactly what she'd been doing. Professor Anderson was going to get the best darn thesis he'd ever seen. As respected as he was, his recommendation would go a long way with any school board in getting her a job. His recommendations were notoriously hard to come by, but she figured she must have already impressed him a little. After all, he had recommended her to the Barneses over all of his other students.

Big deal.

With a heavy sigh, she glanced out the window. The slats of the oak shutters covering it looked like bars. Just look where that recommendation had gotten her. Staid and stiff Professor Anderson would probably choke on his well-modulated vowels if he ever found out what kind of people the Barneses really were. Upstanding members of the community indeed!

That train of thought was derailing her purpose. Resolutely pulling a volume entitled *Art; 1855-1886* across the desk, she began rechecking her notes.

"You really are working in here."

Her pulse skipped, as did her pen when it slid off the edge of the paper. Easy, she warned herself. Just act normal. Creed might be an excellent detective, but even Sherlock Holmes couldn't detect a hidden emotion. "Of course I am!"

"Normal," she thought, was a relative term.

"You don't have to bite my head off."

She swallowed back a rush of irritation—at herself. "Sorry," she muttered, keeping her head bent over the book.

From beneath her lashes her eyes flicked from the well-worn running shoes moving silently over the Sarouk rug, up the sinewy length of hairy legs then quickly over a pair of gray jogging shorts and sleeveless gray sweatshirt. When her veiled glance reached the crew neckline, she jerked her eyes back down.

She'd yet to see him in anything but the most casual clothes and couldn't help but wonder if he hadn't packed anything more formal in that leather bag of his. She assumed it was the same bag he'd planned on taking on his vacation. Certainly his mother wouldn't approve of his running around the Swiss Embassy dressed like that.

"What's the frown for?"

"I didn't know I was frowning."

His deep chuckle sounded tight. "You are."

Making a conscious effort to smooth her brow, she finally looked up at him. He'd stopped beside her and was leaning against the desk scanning the books and papers piled in front of her. "Did you want something?" she inquired guardedly.

He did. He wanted answers. And though she was obviously trying to mask it, Britt was already on the defensive. The best way to skirt that posturing was to get her to relax, then—and how he hated the phrase—hone in for the kill. "You know—" almost hesitantly he reached over and tucked a strand of mahogany hair behind her ear "—you never have told me what your thesis is about."

Her smile, tentative as it was, cloaked the tumult of sensation his gentle touch evoked—and her puzzlement over the bleakness in his eyes. He seemed awfully tense, but she figured she might only be perceiving her own tension in him. "Do you really want to hear about it?" The skeptical arch of her eyebrow lowered. "Or are you just getting bored?"

"Are you saying that a lowly cop can't appreciate something like art history?"

Appalled at his assumption, she vigorously shook her head. "I'm not saying anything of the kind. I just thought you . . ."

"Weren't really interested?" he offered.

"Something like that."

"Well, I am interested. So, are you going to tell me about it or not?"

Not wholly convinced that he wasn't doing this for something to keep himself from going stir-crazy—a person could only read the paper and lay by the pool for so long—she proceeded to explain her theory of how the impressionistic era came into being. If nothing else, she was grateful for the neutral subject. It made coping with his presence a little easier. Not much, but a little.

While Creed wasn't exactly hanging on her every word, he was listening. "Then your purpose is to show how much influence artists like Degas and Cezanne had on each other?" he asked with a rather scholarly look of thoughtfulness.

"Exactly," she returned, pleased. "The influence wasn't just professional, I think it was there on a personal level, too. That's part of what I found so interesting about this. Take Cezanne, for instance. He came from a cultivated, bourgeois background. He even had a law degree. But he was a reverse snob, completely defiant and sometimes downright crude. His peers, artists like Manet and Degas, were quite proper, yet they all used to spend hours together at the Café Guerboise in Paris, discussing their philosophies.''

As Britt continued, Creed kept forgetting the reason he'd interrupted her and found himself becoming more and more enthralled with the sound of her voice, the delicate curve of her throat when she tilted her head, and the way her hands would move to express her thoughts. Then, just as he would find himself imagining the number of little boys who would develop intense crushes on any teacher who looked and sounded like that, he'd remind himself of what he had to do and jerk himself back to reality.

''I guess they were really just a bunch of budding radicals,'' she was saying. ''One historian even spoke of the emergence of a 'generation of radicals in art, lovers of experimental truth.' They were trying something new, expressing their world through impressions rather than stark reality.''

Creed hadn't meant to interrupt, but something she'd just said afforded an opportunity he couldn't let pass. Britt's observations about the artists she spoke of seemed to reflect some of her own personality. Hating himself for the suspicion lurking in his mind, he tried to sound casual. ''Do you believe in experimental truth, Britt?''

Cut off in midsentence, and still immersed in her passion for her favorite subject, she could only answer, ''Of course. It served a very expressive purpose. Picasso...''

''I didn't think he was an impressionist.''

''He wasn't. He never locked himself into any one style or movement.''

''Do you think this experimental truth you were talking about serves any other purpose?''

Something in his hooded eyes warned her. "I think that depends on what you're talking about. Why do I have the feeling we're not discussing art anymore?"

"Probably because we're not."

"Would you mind telling me what we are talking about, then?"

The agitation she'd all but forgotten while she'd been engaged in their mostly one-sided conversation manifested itself in the unconscious twisting of her hands. She locked her fingers together when she saw Creed watching the way she was pleating the fabric of her slacks between them.

"I'm talking about truth," he clarified, his tone quiet and even. "Plain old honesty. Have you been honest with me?"

That uncomfortable knot was back in her stomach again. "Of course I have."

His tone grew quieter. "You're lying."

Enormous brown eyes fixed on his untelling expression. "I am not!"

He wasn't handling this well. She was getting defensive again. "You are, too," he countered softly. "You're hiding something. You've been hiding it ever since this morning when you went tearing out of the house after you thought I'd gone upstairs to shower. Why were you in such a hurry to get out of here?"

All he wanted to do was gather her in his arms, lose his doubts in her softness. He remained perched on the edge of the desk though, his muscles aching at the way he was holding himself back, and waited for something to betray her.

It did. In a split second, she'd jerked her widening eyes from his and a guilty flush rose up the column of her neck.

Creed's heart seemed to stop beating.

Britt's heart slid to her throat. So much for Sherlock.

Chapter Nine

It took several seconds for the shock of Creed's words to wear off; several more for her to regain the composure that had faltered so badly. Now was not the time to overreact. He couldn't possibly know what she was trying to hide. Could he?

"Answer me, Britt."

Certain her secret was safe, even from the eyes that always saw too much, she carefully smoothed the creases she'd folded in her slacks. "What was the question?"

"I asked why you were in such a hurry to get out of the house this morning," he repeated.

Lifting herself gracefully from the depths of her chair, she moved to the credenza beneath the window. Absently she ran her fingers over the polished surface. "I just needed to get outside for a while."

"Any particular reason?"

"Because this place was beginning to get to me." That response was honest, even if it did omit a few details. A restrained smile curved her lips when she glanced over at him. "If you're starting to interrogate me about something as dumb as this, it must be getting to you, too."

She was groping for the more comfortable mood that had settled between them last night while they were playing chess—the light banter that had ensued after the sensual electricity had finally died down to more manageable proportions. She was also trying to change the subject.

Creed wasn't cooperating. "As dumb as what?"

"Really, Creed," she sighed, teasing. "As dumb as why I wanted to go for a walk."

"Why did you want to go for a walk?"

His lack of expression erased her indulgent smile. "I already told you."

"Because you needed to get outside?"

"Yes!"

"Why so defensive all of a sudden?"

"Why these stupid questions?"

"Don't answer a question with a question, Britt." Seeming quite unperturbed, he thumbed through the book she'd abandoned. "Nice pictures," he observed blandly, closing the cover and crossing his arms. Then, in the same dry tone, "I want you to tell me what you're hiding."

And *that* was what was making her so defensive.

Turning from his inscrutable expression, she frowned at the slats of the shutters and tried to force some objectivity into their puzzling exchange. There had to be a reason for his insistence.

Anticipation joined uncertainty. Was it possible he felt something he couldn't admit until he was sure of her? It made sense that a man whose life was ruled by caution and skepticism would want to know where he stood before making himself vulnerable. She could certainly understand that need. No one invited rejection, and she felt far too vulnerable already.

The feel of his hands on her shoulders wasn't helping much. "You can't keep it from me," he assured, turning her to face him. His fingers snaked toward a long, waving curl. Immediately checking himself, he moved his hand back to her shoulder. "Whether you like it or not, we're going to get to the bottom of this. For starters, you can explain what you were doing when you ran into the woods."

She didn't know what that had to do with anything, but she'd play this his way. They always did things his way, anyhow.

Obviously he'd been watching her this morning. Since nothing seemed to escape his notice, he must also be aware of how foolish she felt at having to tell him what she'd been doing. "I..." She swallowed and tried again. The way his thumb was moving over the pulse of her throat was terribly distracting. "I was chasing a squirrel. Not very dignified, huh?"

Her self-mockery was ignored. "A squirrel," he repeated, making it sound as if she'd just invented some mythical, woodland creature.

Willing herself not to react to the way he'd jerked his hands away, she could only guess at the reason for his distrustful scowl. "A squirrel," she reiterated. "It's a furry little brown thing that eats nuts and..."

His teeth clenched, making his interruption a harsh hiss. "Stop lying."

"I'm not lying! They do eat nuts!" What a stupid thing to be arguing about!

"That's not what I mean and you know it."

"I don't, either, and don't call me a liar."

"Then start telling me the truth."

Indignation encountered confusion. "About what?"

"About what you're trying to hide!"

She could only stare at him as he glared back at her. He looked very much like someone who already had the answers and was only asking the questions as a formality. The awful part of that very revealing manifestation was that he seemed quite disgusted with his knowledge.

Lowering her eyes so he couldn't see the pain he was inflicting, she whispered, "I can't," and immediately regretted the words she'd only meant to think. There was no way she could deny she was trying to keep something from him after saying that. She couldn't come out and say she loved him, either, especially with him looking at her that way.

Britt turned to the window, distractedly toying with the collar of her blouse. For long seconds Creed stared at her back, willing his mind to disassociate itself from his heart. When he finally spoke, his voice was as tight as his grip on the back of the wing chair. "Why can't you tell me?"

The man was giving a whole new meaning to persistence. "Because nothing like this has ever happened to me before and, since it's my problem, I can't see any point in discussing it with you."

"I don't care if you see the point or not," he countered. "You're in over your head."

He wasn't going to get any argument on that score. She was in over her head. But she wasn't going down without taking her pride with her. "I don't think you've got a whole lot to say about it," she informed him evenly. He didn't have to accept her love, but he certainly couldn't stop the emotion.

On the other hand, he could definitely test it.

Stepping in front of her, he neatly blocked what she'd hoped would be a dignified exit. "I have everything to say about it, Britt. Especially since I have a pretty good idea of what you're not telling me."

She'd had that feeling all along. Hearing him admit it only made her feel worse.

Apparently he wasn't satisfied to just leave her perched on the edge of the void her heart was plunging toward. He wanted to push her over. "Can't you see it's wrong?"

There was a bleakness in his eyes where only stubbornness had been before. A plea that seemed to beg her to understand.

All she understood was that he didn't want her to love him. "No, Creed," she returned, with a proud tilt to her head. "It may not be very provident or practical, and you may not like it, but I can't see where it's wrong."

Sweeping past him, she started for the entry. She'd barely reached the study doors when his quiet demand stopped her. "Where are you going?"

She hadn't really thought about it. An exit had just seemed more mandatory than ever after that eloquent little speech. Since she was heading for the stairs, she called back, "My room."

"Stay down here."

With that tersely delivered order, he headed for the living room. Britt closed herself in the study, too busy acting as if she wasn't falling apart inside to argue.

For the next hour, Britt vacillated between thoughts of just curling up on the sofa with her misery, and marching in to Creed and demanding to know why her loving him was so wrong. She decided she didn't have the right mental makeup to do the latter. Curiosity was one thing. Masochism was another.

Whatever his reasons, he was now doing his level best to appear as unlovable as possible. Though their encounters were few, their words brief, she could almost feel his irritation every time she saw him.

"It's after two," he announced at one point from the doorway of the study. "Do you want some lunch?"

"No, thanks," she responded coolly, pretending an intense interest in the index cards she was shuffling.

Creed shrugged, leaving nothing but the chill she'd heard in his voice as he walked away.

Another hour dragged by. The phone rang, unnervingly shrill in the deafening quiet. Britt prayed fervently that it would be the long, awaited call from Mr. Barnes. The call that might finally put an end to all this. She prayed just as fervently that it wouldn't be her mother. That was one conversation she simply wasn't up to right now.

The call was for Creed.

She tried to work, but the effort was wasted. The simplest task she could find—alphabetizing her bibliography—was beyond her ability to concentrate. All she was doing was making mistakes that would have to be corrected later. Her head hurt. Her stomach was in knots. And she couldn't begin to comprehend Creed's attitude.

Swiveling her chair around, her eyes skimmed over the floor-to-ceiling bookcase. There weren't any titles in the row of books hiding the wall safe that dealt with the subject of how to understand your warden, so she tried some rationale of her own. Maybe now that her mother had left, he was treating her as he would any other suspect in this situation. Her mother's presence had necessitated a closeness between them he obviously didn't feel and . . .

That logic wasn't worth dwelling on. Even before her mother had shown up, he hadn't treated her quite like this.

Pressing her fingers to the dull throb in her temples, she tried to blank her mind. Thinking wasn't helping at all. She needed to do something. Pacing seemed appropriate.

By the time she decided that the only thing that would help her headache was food, the sun was hanging like a great orange ball above the hills. Her pacing had brought her to the window and her eyes swept along the tops of the trees. The wispy clouds were infused with tints of pink, lavender and mauve, the pale pastels perfectly complementing the blue of the sky. A Monet sunset, she mused, aware that for about three whole seconds she'd been thinking of something other than Creed.

Turning from the spectacular display, she moved quietly to the entry and peeked into the living room. Creed was lying on the sofa watching television, only the top of his head visible on its arm. He didn't move when she ventured another step.

So far, so good, she commended herself a few minutes later, keeping an eye on the louvered door. After downing the aspirin she'd retrieved from the bathroom, she'd made herself a peanut butter sandwich and poured a glass of milk. The meal was far from substantial, but she hadn't wanted to risk drawing Creed's attention with the clatter of pots and pans. She couldn't bear another of his disapproving glares.

The brilliant sunset beckoned. Instead of returning to the four walls of the study, she plopped her sandwich on a paper towel, picked up her milk, and started for the back door. With any amount of luck, she could eat her dinner in peace.

No luck.

"Just where do you think you're sneaking off to?"

The dull ache in her head escalated to a pounding throb at Creed's insolent inquiry. "I'm not sneaking anywhere," she sighed, turning to see his narrowed eyes move from her uncut sandwich to the paleness of her strained features. "I was only going out to the patio."

Leaning toward the counter, he folded his arms over his gray sweatshirt and nodded toward the breakfast nook. "Eat in here."

"I'd really rather..."

"I said, eat in here."

Enough was enough. Curbing the urge to throw her meal down on the counter—or at him—she set it down carefully, and winced at the pain slicing through her head when she jerked back to face him. She didn't have the nerve to ask all the questions plaguing her, but there was one she had to have answered. "Why are you treating me like this?"

The look she bestowed on his maddeningly arrogant expression was considerably less effective than she wanted. It was impossible to look quelling when your heart was breaking and your head felt as if it was about to explode.

All Creed saw behind that ineffective attempt at control was the pleading brown eyes that lacked the spark he'd seen so often before. "I'm treating you the only way I can right now," he returned, noting the tremor in her fingers when she pressed them to her temples.

She'd seemed a little pale a few moments ago. Now the delicate contours of her face looked almost haunted, and her skin as white as a snowbank. Her long lashes fluttered down as she turned away, allowing him only a glimpse of the hurt he'd seen in her eyes. There seemed to be more to that hurt than just a headache.

Lacking the defiance he'd come to expect when she was being ordered around, she picked up her glass of milk. "I'll go back in the study."

"Why don't you take some aspirin?"

"I already did."

"Go upstairs and lie down, then."

Still none of the expected rebellion. Just a quiet "I will" before she slipped through the louvered doors.

Crossing the kitchen, Creed picked up the sandwich she'd made for herself. A string of profound curses followed it in an arc to the sink.

Sick of the ambivalence gnawing at him—damn all those years of training that made him suspect her every move—he bounded toward the stairs. Until this morning, he'd thought her so open, and honest to a fault. Now he was questioning everything she'd ever said or done. She'd faked their "engagement" so well that even her own mother, someone who should know her better than anyone else, had been convinced. Had Britt been faking the physical responses he'd felt in her, too?

Gripping the banister to keep from storming into her room like some raging maniac, he fought for a sense of detachment—that professional indifference that had always served him so well.

It was impossible. He couldn't disassociate himself any more. The part of him that insisted on denying the cool logic of evidence—circumstantial as it was—wanted only to make her trust him. Gaining her trust demanded patience. He'd be gentle. He'd coax.

He'd wring her beautiful neck.

She hadn't closed her door. The glass of milk she'd brought up sat untouched on the nightstand and a soft evening breeze was fluttering the drapes of her open window. Britt was nowhere to be seen.

At least he didn't see her until she emerged from her bathroom with a wash cloth pressed to her forehead.

The relief he felt at having his worst suspicions so innocently rebuked must have been plainly visible—if the odd expression furrowing her brow when she glanced at him was any indication. She said nothing and lowered herself to the edge of the bed.

"Pretty bad, huh?" He was referring to her headache. He had one himself, though it was more figurative than literal.

"Lousy," she expanded, looking as if she wanted to lie down but wasn't sure she should with him in the room.

He inclined his head toward the window. "Does the fresh air help?"

"I don't know yet. It's too soon to tell."

Picking up the silky nightshirt he'd held her in last night, he tossed it to the foot of the bed and sat down beside her. She stiffened. "Relax for a minute," he said soothingly, pushing her hair from the back of her neck. "If you tense up, it'll only make your head hurt more. Someone showed me the nerve points to press—" the pads of his fingers stroked slowly above her ears "—and it always works for me."

Her head lolled forward. Resting her elbows on her knees, she pressed the cool cloth over her eyes. He couldn't help thinking that she must really be hurting to give in to a massage this easily. He'd thought for sure she'd tell him to leave.

"Just don't start yelling at me again," she sighed.

"I promise not to yell, if you'll level with me." The muscles in her neck grew perceptibly tighter. "Don't do that," he admonished, pushing her shoulders down to resume his gentle probing. "I want you to relax so we can talk."

"I don't feel like talking."

"Then just listen, and nod yes or no. And please, Britt—" he peeled back the edge of the cloth so he could see her eyes . . . one eye anyway "—be honest with me."

She pushed the cloth back up and mumbled into her palms. "I've always been honest with you."

She had no idea how much he wanted to believe that. "Do you remember what we were talking about this morning?" He didn't think she'd forgotten. But instead of the expected nod, she shrugged off his hands, pulled herself to her feet and dropped the cloth on the nightstand.

"Of course I remember." Her response was faint, sounding more like she was talking to herself than to him. "I just wish Mr. Barnes would call so this whole thing would be over with."

Wondering at the defeat in her tone, the dejection in her stance, Creed gripped his hands between his knees. "Is that the signal you're waiting for?"

His quiet question was met with her unblinking stare.

He tried again, adopting a different approach. Though he was only doing his job, he hated having to resort to this kind of accusation. "Was that what you were doing this morning? Leaving a note for your accomplice telling him Barnes hadn't called yet?" As her mouth fell open, he placed himself squarely in front of her. "You're supposed to deliver the money to him, aren't you? That's why he's waiting out there."

Her eyes were widening. She could feel them taking on the circumference of tea saucers. The thought prompting that reaction hit her so forcefully she forgot to deny what he'd just said. He hadn't been treating her like a pariah all day because he didn't want her love. He didn't even know how she felt. He'd been treating her like this because he thought she was involved with the Barneses after all.

"Who is he, Britt?" Creed was demanding. "Who did you signal from your window?"

Still reeling from the jolt of what she'd just realized, she snapped, "I didn't signal anybody," and wished she'd managed a quieter tone. The one she'd used made her head feel like the inside of an echo chamber.

The certainty he could see flashing in her eyes would have convinced him she was telling the truth if he hadn't seen what she'd done himself. "You mean to tell me you don't know anything about the guy out there? What were you doing? Waving at your squirrel?"

Drawing a shaky hand through her curls, and knowing how horribly misconstrued the situation had become, she slowly shook her head. "Creed, I really don't know what's going on here." Something else hit her. Something equally unsettling. "There's someone besides your team out there?"

Her tremorous question remained unanswered. "Tell me whom you signaled from your window."

The Inquisitor. That's whom his accusing stance reminded her of. Dark. Forboding. Ominous. "I didn't signal anyone," she repeated, then remembered the figure moving between the trees. "Your man. One of your men was watching from the woods and I waved at him. But that's the only person I saw and I wasn't signaling..."

"That wasn't my man. What did you go racing into the woods for?"

A new sense of unease crept through her as she lowered herself into the chair. She felt very much like she had back at the station when the officer had been questioning her. Afraid. "I told you before. I was going crazy. I had to get out of here."

In her present state of mind, his movement toward her seemed almost menacing. "This morning, when I met you in the kitchen and when you came back inside, you were agitated. Evasive. You didn't try to deny that you were hiding something, either. If you didn't know he was out there and weren't trying to keep that from me, then what were you trying to hide?"

He was standing over her now, his gray-blue eyes pinning her back to the chair. The beat of her heart echoed the pounding in her head. "It wasn't anything about..."

"Don't tell me what it isn't," he growled, clamping his hands on the arms of the chair. He brought his face to within inches of hers. "Tell me what it is."

If her head hadn't been hurting so badly, if his manner hadn't been so irritatingly intimidating, she might have debated the necessity of answering him. Was it more important to preserve her integrity, or her pride? Already having suffered his rejection, however prematurely, she figured things couldn't get much worse, and banished the question. "I thought you knew I was in love with you," she heard herself saying.

His whole body seemed to slack before he jerked himself away. "You what?" came the quietly incredulous question from above her.

She'd spoken so softly that Creed knew he couldn't possibly have heard correctly. But when she repeated what she'd said, he trained his eyes on the floor, needing visible proof that it was still beneath his feet.

He turned away when she cautiously raised her eyes, certain his ability to mask his reaction had failed him completely. The last thing he'd expected to hear just then was an admission of love. Certainly not in the context of what they'd been discussing—or, what he'd thought they'd been discussing.

Slanting a guarded glance over his shoulder, he raked his fingers through his hair. He didn't know what to say.

Either she was the epitome of innocence, in every possible interpretation of the word, or the world's best actress. Having found himself thoroughly enmeshed in her spell, he didn't know what to believe anymore. Her flimsy story about the squirrel was just crazy enough to be true. Crazier than that was the urge—the need—to tell her he loved her, too. He'd never said those words to anyone in his life and if he didn't get out of here right now...

"Creed?" The plea in her voice drew his eyes to her. "You believe me, don't you? About that...that man, I mean?"

His voice broke slightly as he reached over to smooth the hair from her face. "I want to. I think you know that." Something tightened in his throat, preventing any further admissions. "Try to rest. We'll talk when you feel better."

Turning from the distress in her too-bright eyes, he headed out the door, his mind and his heart locked in a siege that threatened to tear him apart. For the first time in his career, he could no longer trust his judgment— professional or otherwise.

Britt moved to her bed, listening to Creed's fading footsteps. She'd never thought of herself as a masochist before, but she was almost grateful for the blinding pain in her head. It made it impossible to think.

She fell asleep, only to awaken with everything she didn't want to think about clamoring around in her mind. At least the headache was gone.

She tried to reclaim the oblivion of unconsciousness again, but her thoughts wouldn't let her. Creed wanted to believe her, but couldn't. And if he couldn't believe her, her couldn't really care for her.

Pulling her pillow over her head, she tried to concentrate on something else. The thought that popped into her mind was just as unsettling as the others. There was a stranger outside hiding in the woods. That gave her the creeps.

Deciding that lying there wouldn't accomplish anything, she swung her feet to the floor. She'd bring her thesis upstairs and try to undo some of the damage she'd wreaked on it earlier. That should keep her mind occupied for a while.

The hem of her blouse had come loose from her slacks and tucking it back in, she opened the door. Creed's door was closed, and the hallway dark. Careful not to make any noise so she wouldn't disturb him, she slipped down the stairs.

Only the rhythmic tick of the grandfather clock in the entry marred the midnight silence. Picking out the shadowy outline of the study's threshold, she moved quietly across the marble floor.

She got no farther than the double doors.

Chapter Ten

An eerie stillness surrounded her. She could hear nothing but the rustle of papers being scattered by the breeze coming through the open window behind the desk. The shutters had been pushed back, a sliver of moonlight illuminating the books tossed haphazardly on the floor—the books that had hidden the wall safe.

The safe. Though she could barely see it, it was open.

All Britt could hear now was the sound of her heart pounding in her ears. Swallowing a rush of pure panic, she whirled around and darted for the stairs. Creed. She had to get Creed.

"Stop her!"

A scream lodged in her throat. Panic had blinded her to the two shadowed figures bolting through the doorway leading from the kitchen. An instant later, she'd slammed against a massive chest.

Struggling against the manaclelike arms locked around her, she barely heard the demand hissed above her head. "What are you doing down here?"

Terror gave way to unutterable relief. Sagging against the solid male frame, she breathed in the familiar spicy scent mingling with the freshness of night air clinging to his shirt. It was Creed's arms stilling her struggles. His voice grating in her ear. She'd thought he was upstairs in his room. What was he doing down here? Who was the huge, dark silhouette darting into the study?

Her mind was forming the questions, but her vocal cords were paralyzed. Only seconds had passed. She was still caught in that debilitating mix of fear and relief and what was happening now only added to that confusion.

A sharp expletive preceded the words shouted from the study. "He got out!"

Creed's terse "Get the light, Hollister" was followed by a clipped "Answer me, damn it" as he gripped her upper arms. It felt as if he was going to shake her.

"It's obvious enough what she was doing," the man Creed had addressed as Hollister pronounced, a blaze of light flooding the entry to reveal his smug expression.

Narrowing her eyes against the sudden brightness, Britt jerked around. A burly bear of a man in a blue sweatshirt had just burst through the front door. "Bronski nailed him in the bushes," he said, grinning. "Man, he was in and out of there so fast..."

"We know," Hollister interrupted. His surly gaze fell on Britt who was trying her best not to collapse against the banister. Creed had pushed her behind him the instant the door flew open. "Either he knew the combination, or someone opened the safe for him."

There was no mistaking the implication. He was accusing her—and the guy in the blue sweatshirt was nodding his agreement.

"No!" The denial seemed torn from her throat. Her eyes locked on Creed's. What she saw there was totally devastating. It was the look of a man whose soul had shattered. A man whose inner torment was almost more than he could bear.

His broad shoulders rose with his deep breath. Lowering his eyes, he turned away. "Bring the other car up, Moss." He was addressing the man in the sweatshirt. "You and Bronski take Miss Chandler. Hollister and I..."

Britt didn't hear the rest of Creed's instructions. Desperation vied with fear, compounding the dull ache in her heart. "I didn't open that safe!"

No one was more surprised than she was by the strength in her voice; strength that seemed to falter as three pairs of male eyes fell on her ashen features. "I only came down to..."

"Be quiet, Britt."

Though the order was delivered calmly, she knew Creed meant it to be obeyed. But there was too much at stake for her to capitulate so easily. "But I didn't..."

"Listen to me for once, will you? Just shut up and don't say anything. Not one word."

What did he want? Not twenty seconds ago he was demanding to know what she was doing down here. Now she was trying to tell him and he was telling her to be quiet!

Moss took off at a dead run—apparently to get the car Creed had been talking about—and a very self-satisfied Hollister was pushing her out the door. He was saying something about her having the right to remain silent, then Creed, his eyes blazing, was jerking Hollister back, telling him, "Go help Bronski." Bronski was apparently the jean-clad officer frisking the tall, skinny guy lying spread-eagle on the hood of Creed's Cadillac.

"Will someone please listen to me?" Her plea was barely audible over the roar of the car coming up the drive. She wasn't sure, but she thought she'd just been arrested. Halfway arrested anyway. Creed hadn't let Hollister finish whatever it was he'd been saying. "I came downstairs to get my thesis..." She was following Creed toward the group clustered around his car. "The window was open when I got to the study and..."

"How is your thesis coming along, Brittany? Have you managed to refute everything I told you about our friend Cezanne?"

Glances darted among the officers, then bounced between Britt's dumbfounded expression and the man now wearing a pair of handcuffs. No one seemed to be paying any attention to the screech of tires and the crackling static of a police radio accompanying Moss's exit from a rather battered-looking green sedan.

Britt's disbelieving eyes had widened perceptibly—both at the way the man had addressed her and at the features now visible beneath his brown stocking cap. Even with the mop of graying blond hair covered up, and without his horn rimmed glasses, she recognized him immediately. "Professor Anderson," she gasped.

Hollister was elbowing his way around Creed, his tone indignant. "There's somebody else involved in this besides you and the Barneses?" he demanded of the Professor. "Who's Cezanne?"

"An artist," Creed clipped, his brooding gaze turning quizzical as it fell on Britt. She was pushing a handful of tousled curls from her face, as if she couldn't quite believe what she was seeing.

"That fits," Hollister grunted to the other officers. "Do we have any leads on him?"

Professor Anderson scowled in scholarly disgust. "Cezanne is dead."

"You saying you got rid of him?"

Exasperation tinged Creed's tone. "He died before you were born. Bronski, get him down to the station before Hollister decides to book him for murder, too."

Moss pushed past Britt, forcing her up against Creed. "I thought you wanted me and Bronski to take her."

"I changed my mind." Creed's hand slid over the back of her blouse. Opening the door of his car, he nudged her into the back seat and tossed his keys to a frowning Hollister. "You drive."

The men were grimly silent during the ride to the station, which left Britt with nothing to do but try to figure out what was going on in their minds. Figuring out Hollister's thoughts was easy enough. He'd insisted to Creed all along that she was guilty and seemed enormously pleased that his opinion was being proven correct. Discerning Creed's thoughts wasn't quite so simple—especially when he reached over and folded his hand over her cold fingers.

Two hours later she was still wondering what had prompted that small gesture of reassurance. The minute they'd set foot inside the station, she'd been turned over to a police matron who'd deposited her on a bench by a group of desks. Creed had muttered something to the matron, but he hadn't said a word to her.

Shifting on the hard wooden seat, and trying her best to appear inconspicuous to the two dozen or so people filling the room, she glanced up to see a group of men and one woman hurrying down the hall. For a moment, the man and woman in the middle of that group looked like John and Henrietta Barnes. That was impossible. They were in Europe.

Or she'd thought they were anyway. She'd also thought that Professor Anderson was in Boston, but that certainly hadn't been the case. Where had they taken him? Where was Creed? How much longer were they going to make her sit here before someone would tell her what was going on?

"Don't look so disappointed," Creed said, casting another impatient glance at his watch. It was almost 3:00 A.M. "I've been wrong about suspects myself."

Following Creed out of the interrogation room, Hollister muttered, "Yeah, but when was the last time you tried to convince your superior that his woman was a con?"

His woman. Even if he'd wanted to deny that's how he felt about Britt, no one would have believed him. When that mushy-mouthed professor said he'd picked her for his pigeon because she was so naive, only Hollister's grip on his shoulder had kept him from going for the jerk's throat. Britt wasn't exactly a hardened sophisticate, but she wasn't naive. She wasn't gullible, either. She just trusted people. The fact that Anderson and the Barneses had abused that trust had made Creed angrier than he'd ever been in his life.

A middle-aged woman was waving a sheaf of papers at him from a few feet away. "I've got the reports typed up, Captain . . . I mean, Chief."

It seemed that no one knew quite what to call him tonight. The new title wouldn't be official for another week, but Creed was so preoccupied, not to mention tired, that he wasn't sure who he was, anyway. "Thanks, Bess," he called back, hurrying toward his destination. "I'll sign 'em later."

"Now, Creed," she coaxed, sounding more like a mother than a clerk. "They have to be signed now."

Muttering a succinct expletive that was quickly followed by a muttered "Sorry," he took the file and ducked inside his office.

It was empty. He'd told that matron to have Britt wait in there, but seeing the tarps draped over everything and the paint cans sitting next to the half-painted walls, he couldn't get too upset over having his order disobeyed. He poked his head back out the door. "Want to get back on my good side, Hollister?"

The detective turned sharply, his eagerness barely hidden by his casual "Sure."

"Go find Britt and tell her what happened. This'll only take me a minute, but I don't want her sitting out there stewing any longer than she has to."

The spot Britt was studying on the floor had just been covered with a pair of tennis shoes. "They've cleared you," their owner said from above her.

Hollister's expression was almost contrite. Britt's was blank. "They?"

"Anderson and the Barneses."

She hated sounding so imbecilic, but all she could seem to manage was, "The Barneses?"

"We picked them up at a motel out on the highway. They were waiting for Anderson to come back with the money. Guess that call we made to his office to check out your story made 'em nervous. You know," he continued with something that looked like an apologetic smile, "if it makes you feel any better, you weren't the first student Anderson used in this scheme. Looks like over the past several years, he and the Barneses used quite a few others."

"I see," she said, not really sure that she did. "Is...is Creed still here?"

Responding with a nod, he cleared his throat. "He just wanted me to tell you everything's okay now."

"I see," she repeated, only this time she did understand. "Thank you."

"Sure thing, Miss Chandler." With that, he gave her a tight little smile and turned down the hall.

So that was it. It was all over now. Just like that. After everything that had happened, the least she'd expected was something a little more climactic than some stranger telling her "everything's okay now." A little relief on her part wouldn't have been out of place. She was free. Her name had been cleared. So what was the matter with her?

The way she'd been used by her professor and his friends had nothing to do with the numb sensation creeping over her. Nor did it have anything to do with the suspicious moisture brimming in her eyes. Creed had sent Hollister instead of coming himself. That could only mean he didn't want to see her again.

Yes, it was all over now. Everything.

Knowing that if she sat there for another second, she'd do something incredibly embarrassing—like burst into tears—she drew herself to her feet. All she had to do was hold her head up and put one foot in front of the other until she reached the doors on the other side of the room. Surely she could manage that.

She had no idea what she'd do once she got outside the door though. She hadn't brought her purse, so she couldn't take a cab. Even if she could get back to the

Barneses' house, she couldn't stay there. Somehow, though, she had to get her clothes and . . .

One of the dozen steps she'd taken was retraced when someone grabbed her arm and pulled her around. An instant later she was staring at a broad expanse of gray sweatshirt.

"Where are you going?" Creed worriedly scanned her drawn features, his fatigue making the question sound like a demand.

Since she wasn't really sure, and the gentle pressure of his hand was making it difficult to be very inventive, she said, "I was just leaving," and felt his fingers tighten. "It's all right, isn't it?" she ventured, suddenly uncertain. Maybe she wasn't supposed to leave yet. "Your detective told me what happened, so I assumed I could . . ."

She didn't get to tell him what she assumed. Taking her by the shoulders, Creed jerked forward to keep her from being run over. Two uniformed officers were trying to squeeze a third person through the narrow aisleway between the desks. "Will you let me talk to you for a minute?" To hell with the paint fumes, he swore to himself. "In my office?"

In her present state of mind, being alone with him didn't seem like such a terrific idea. The past few hours had taken their toll and she was too tired to keep her emotions beneath the surface. It would be simpler to just say their goodbyes right here. "Creed, I really appreciate . . . I mean, thank you for . . ." Oh, good grief, she groaned to herself. What was she trying to say anyway? Under the circumstances saying "thanks for everything" would only sound sarcastic. She settled for something that didn't require any verbal finesse. "Could you lend me a few dollars?"

His black eyebrows formed a single slash. "What for?"

"A cab."

"You don't need a cab."

"How am I supposed to get my stuff from the house, then?"

"Britt," he sighed. "Can't we talk about this somewhere a little more private?"

"Why do we need privacy to discuss my transportation?"

"That's not what I want to discuss." He hesitated, his eyes darting around the crowded room. "This isn't the place to talk," he growled, "but nothing about us has been normal so far, so I suppose it's about par for the course." Ignoring the curious glances being tossed in their direction, he pulled her between a row of tall file cabinets, and cradled her face between his hands. For about three seconds, he didn't do anything but stare down at the velvety brown eyes that couldn't seem to move from his. "I've got to know," he whispered, his face inches from hers. "Did you mean it when you said you loved me?"

Unprepared for his question, for the plea in his voice, she just stared up at him and tried to comprehend what was happening. A quiet anxiety marked his expression, a perfect mirror of her own precarious emotions. And in his touch she could feel his tension increase while he waited for her response.

The weariness she'd been fighting was forgotten, along with all the hurt and doubt that had carried her up to this moment. "Not loved," she refuted gently, touching the back of his hand. "That makes it sound like something in the past."

"Meaning that what you feel has a present and a future? As in, I love you, Britt?"

Somehow, he'd pulled her closer. His hands had anchored themselves in her hair. "You do?" she whispered.

"More than I ever thought possible. Oh, babe," he groaned, his arms enveloping her so tightly she could barely breathe, "you have no idea what I've gone through the past twenty-four hours. It seemed like one minute I was trying to figure out ways to convince you that Portland needed art history teachers and the next I was trying to figure out what kind of work I could do in Switzerland. I didn't know if I was going to take you and leave the country, or spend weekends visiting the state pen. Can you imagine how that would look? You can't believe the crazy things I thought about doing."

She pulled back, as far as his arms would allow anyway. People were craning their necks to see what was going on between the file cabinets, but she didn't care. All she cared about was the man who would have given up everything for her. "Things got a little messed up, didn't they?"

Chuckling at her understatement, he gave the curl touching her collar a gentle yank. "A little, and now that things are getting straightened out, we've got another detail to take care of."

If the intent in his eyes as his head lowered was any indication, she had a pretty good idea of what that detail was. Curving her arms around his neck, she decided to ask anyway. "What's that?"

"We've got to see the District Attorney," he mumbled against her mouth, and when she tried to pull back, he pinned her against him and deepened the kiss. If he'd noticed that the noise level in the room had dropped considerably, he was doing his best to ignore it.

"What do we have to see him for?" she finally was able to ask, though her voice had a decidedly husky quality to it.

"I need to ask him if he'll be available to go to Boston. Your mother already thinks there's going to be a wedding, so I guess I'll need a best man."

He was right. They should have had this discussion someplace else. "Are you sure?"

"Of course I am. Every wedding I've ever been to had a best..."

"No! About..."

"Getting married?" His smile faltered when he saw the doubt flickering through her eyes. "Aren't you?"

She was sure. She'd never been more certain of anything in her life. To spend the rest of her days as Creed's wife, the mother of his children, his friend... "It's just that we've only known each other for six days."

"Seven, if you count the day we met as day one. And that's more than enough time for me. I come from a long line of short engagements. Mom and Dad only knew each other for three days before they got married. Uncle Alex met Aunt Katrin on a Sunday and they were married the following Friday. Grandma Alice took a little longer though, she and my grandfather took almost a month, but a cousin on Dad's side..."

"Okay," she laughed, letting her fingers slip through the dark curls at the back of his head. "I get the picture." Another picture slipped into place. Both she and Creed had curly hair. Their kids didn't stand a chance.

"That's a relief," he said with a sigh that sounded quite genuine. "Family tradition is very important, you know . . . and it really would be a shame to ruin all your mom's plans."

"A terrible shame," she agreed, drawing his head down to meet her lips.

It was probably just her imagination, but the thundering in her ears sounded strangely like applause.

Silhouette Romance

COMING NEXT MONTH

CHAMPAGNE GIRL—Diana Palmer
Underneath Catherine's bubbly facade, there was much more to the champagne girl. But could she leave Matt and her home in Texas for a job in the bright city lights of New York?

LAUGHTER IN THE RAIN—Debbie Macomber
Although Abby loved Logan, she would still dream about storybook romance. Tate seemed to walk right out of the pages—but how long can you hold on to a dream?

THE PAINTED VEIL—Elizabeth Hunter
Thirsa hid her emotions behind her painting. It brought great artistic success . . . but left little room for romance. Until Luis Kirkpatrick. The painter could see her soul—and share her deepest desires.

HERO IN BLUE—Terri McGraw
Tara was an attorney fighting her first case as public defender. She was determined not to mix business with pleasure, but Lieutenant Dan DeAngelo was putting her heart under arrest.

GETTING PHYSICAL—Marie Nicole
Rory had to compete in a minitriathlon to inherit her late uncle's physical fitness empire. Zak was thrilled to help her train—and show her the fitness of getting physical . . . with him!

SWEET MOCKINGBIRD'S CALL—Emilie Richards
More romance among the MacDonald clan, that fun-loving family you read about in *Sweet Georgia Gal*. Find out what happens to Wendy and Shane . . . would their childhood love endure after seven years?

AVAILABLE NOW:

THE INFAMOUS MADAM X
Joan Smith

LOOKALIKE LOVE
Nancy John

IRISH EYES
Lynnette Morland

DARLING DETECTIVE
Karen Young

TALL, DARK AND HANDSOME
Glenda Sands

STOLEN PROMISE
Christine Flynn

Silhouette Special Edition

AMERICAN ✦ TRIBUTE

AMERICAN TRIBUTE

Where a man's dreams count for more than his parentage...

Look for these upcoming titles under the Special Edition American Tribute banner.

CHEROKEE FIRE
Gena Dalton #307—May 1986
It was Sabrina Dante's silver spoon that Cherokee cowboy Jarod Redfeather couldn't trust. The two lovers came from opposite worlds, but Jarod's Indian heritage taught them to overcome their differences.

NOBODY'S FOOL
Renee Roszel #313—June 1986
Everyone bet that Martin Dante and Cara Torrence would get together. But Martin wasn't putting any money down, and Cara was out to prove that she was nobody's fool.

MISTY MORNINGS, MAGIC NIGHTS
Ada Steward #319—July 1986
The last thing Carole Stockton wanted was to fall in love with another politician, especially Donnelly Wakefield. But under a blanket of secrecy, far from the campaign spotlights, their love became a powerful force.

AM-TRIB-1R

Silhouette Special Edition

AMERICAN TRIBUTE

*American Tribute titles
now available:*

RIGHT BEHIND THE RAIN
Elaine Camp #301–April 1986
The difficulty of coping with her brother's
death brought reporter Raleigh Torrence
to the office of Evan Younger, a police
psychologist. He helped her to deal with
her feelings and emotions, including love.

THIS LONG WINTER PAST
Jeanne Stephens #295–March 1986
Detective Cody Wakefield checked out
Assistant District Attorney Liann McDowell,
but only in his leisure time. For it was the
danger of Cody's job that caused Liann to
shy away.

LOVE'S HAUNTING REFRAIN
Ada Steward #289–February 1986
For thirty years a deep dark secret kept them
apart—King Stockton made his millions while
his wife, Amelia, held everything together.
Now could they tell their secret, could they
admit their love?

OFFICIAL SWEEPSTAKES INFORMATION

1. **NO PURCHASE NECESSARY.** To enter, complete the official entry/order form. Be sure to indicate whether or not you wish to take advantage of our subscription offer.

2. Entry blanks have been pre-selected for the prizes offered. Your response will be checked to see if you are a winner. In the event that these are not claimed, a random drawing will be held from all entries received to award not less than $150,000 in prizes. This is in addition to any free, surprise or mystery gifts which might be offered. Versions of this sweepstakes with different prizes will appear in Torstar Ltd. mailings and their affiliates. Winners selected will receive the prize offered in their sweepstakes insert.

3. This promotion is being conducted under the supervision of Marden-Kane, an independent judging organization. By entering the sweepstakes, each entrant accepts and agrees to be bound by these rules and the decisions of the judges which shall be final and binding. Odds of winning in the random drawing are dependent upon the total number of entries received. Taxes, if any, are the sole responsibility of the prize winners. Prizes are non-transferable. All entries must be received by August 31, 1986.

4. This sweepstakes package offers:

1, Grand Prize	: Cruise around the world on the QEII	$100,000 total value
4, First Prizes	: Set of matching pearl necklace and earrings	$ 20,000 total value
10, Second Prizes	: Romantic Weekend in Bermuda	$ 15,000 total value
25, Third Prizes	: Designer Luggage	$ 10,000 total value
200, Fourth Prizes	: $25 Gift Certificate	$ 5,000 total value
		$150,000

Winners may elect to receive the cash equivalent for the prizes offered.

5. This offer is open to residents of the U.S. and Canada, 18 years and older, except employees of Torstar Ltd., its affiliates, subsidiaries, Marden-Kane and all other agencies and persons connected with conducting this sweepstakes. All Federal, State and local laws apply. Void in the province of Quebec and wherever prohibited or restricted by law. Winners will be notified by mail and may be required to execute an affidavit of eligibility and release which must be returned within 14 days after notification. Canadian winners will be required to answer a skill testing question. Winners consent to the use of their names, photograph and/or likeness for advertising and publicity purposes in conjunction with this and similar promotions without additional compensation. One prize per family or household.

6. For a list of our most current prize winners, send a stamped, self-addressed envelope to: WINNERS LIST, c/o Marden-Kane, P.O. Box 10404, Long Island City, New York 11101.